PRAISE FOR KAYE PARK HINCKLEY'S *BIRDS OF A FEATHER*

Kaye Park ... ... yle
made famo... by ... ...ibed
our flawed nature. ... ...icles broken
individuals ... their sea... ... ... the reader is
delighted by the ... ...hallenged to
examine th... longing of ... ...rns
about faith... As Kaye writes in her debut novel, *A Hunger* *in*
the Heart, "All you have to do is reach out for her. Love will
reach back. Love alw... ...

—Dr. Ron O'Gorm...

There are plenty of ... ... act that
they have written ... ...wn for
short stories. In rece... ... ...eared in
the American South. No, I'm not talking about Flannery
O'Connor, much as I enjoy her work. I'm talking today about
Kaye Park Hinckley, whose debut novel, *A Hunger in the*
Heart, came out in 2013. She has now given us a collection of
short stories. As with her novel, Kaye explores the human soul
with all its potential for beauty and hideousness, strength and
weakness: we see lust, greed, ambition and hatred. But we also
see wisdom and fidelity, love and loyalty, repentance and
redemption. Hinckley examines life in all its stages: birth,
marriage, youth, parenthood, old age, and death.

—Richard Van Holst,
Redeemer University College in Ancaster, Ontario, Canada

Kaye Park Hinckley revives Flannery O'Connor's Christ-
haunted South in this compelling collection. I was intrigued by
"The Psalm of David Fowler," and "The Mercy Seat." Truly we
are all birds of a feather trying to make our way through our
faults which we would rather ignore until we are struck by a
moment of amazing grace. Amazed that the sinner lawyer in
"Red Bird" blissfully moved to... ... ...death while his
unforgiving wife seem tortured to t... ... ...
forgive. "Shooting at Heaven's Ga... ...
—Mike Sullivan, Founder of the ...
Assistant District Attorney, Tuscaloo...

Good stuff. A solid book. Several of us in the Florida First Coast Writers' Festival tracked the writing progress of Kaye Park Hinckley, and we're delighted to see that our alumna has published a short story collection. In *Birds of a Feather,* readers will find keen insights into dramas set in the Florida Panhandle, South Alabama, and the Tuscaloosa-Birmingham region, [including] a ghost story that provides a different spin on the post-Civil War life.

—William Howard Denson III, Humanities-English professor (ret.), Florida State College at Jacksonville.
Author of *Mowbray and the Sharks,* and others.

While certainly different in context, language, and approach, these stories express faith in the same manner employed by Flannery O'Connor. Having previously read this author in novel form, I must say I think the short story form is an even greater strength. Gritty tones in places, sweet dispositions on display in others. I can't say enough good.

—Josh Webber, Murfreesboro, TN

In this fine story collection, Kaye Park Hinckley leaves no doubt that she is a theologian of the cross . . . You won't find this kind of hard-core realism in the "Christian Fiction" section at Barnes and Noble where theologians of glory are cashing in big these days. Here are dope fiend lunatics, adulterers, and drunks, along with hard working, sympathetic, normal folks.

—Jim Hale, Manakin Sabot, VA

Birds of a Feather

Kaye Park Hinckley

Birds of a Feather

Kaye Park Hinckley

Wiseblood Books

Milwaukee, Wisconsin

Printed in the United States of America
Set in Arabic Typesetting

Library of Congress Cataloging-in-Publication Data
Hinckley, Kaye Park, 1944-
Birds of a Feather/ Kaye Park Hinckley;
1. Hinckley, Kaye Park, 1944-
2. Fiction

ISBN-13: 978-0692234730
ISBN-10: 069223473X

7/12/16

NG

SIG

BIRDS OF A FEATHER

Kaye Park Hinckley

For my husband, George, the father of our children
and the keeper of my heart.

TABLE OF CONTENTS

Red Bird

The recurring dream has been with Jude for thirty years, nearly half his life. In it, he's a boy of six or seven, cornered by an elderly man in a wrinkled linen suit and a white straw hat. The man has caught him in the act of —he doesn't know exactly what, because this is where the dream always begins. It could be a number of things. Jude isn't sure if the man is friend or enemy. The man never speaks, only passes judgment with his eyes.

By now, Jude is used to the dream, to the old man and his quiet condemnation. When the large hand reaches for him, he usually shrinks to nothing then wakes with a sense of accomplishment that he has out-smarted his judge another time. But when he wakes this November morning, he doesn't remember having dreamed at all. Something different muddles his mind, some confusion he can't get rid of.

A drizzle of rain, in the rhythm of a heart-beat, taps against his bedroom window. He turns to look, but the corner of the down pillow is flipped up and blocks his vision. He raises a weak hand to pat it down, surprised at how much strength diabetes has stolen from him. The gray sky appears disfigured by an arthritic tree and a cardinal clings to a leafless limb, a red blemish in the drizzling rain. He's not sure why he shouts, "Get away, red bird. Fly before you're caught!"

Disturbed footsteps come fast down the hall. His wife, Carolyn, peeks curiously into the room, but he pretends he is sleeping. She takes a labored breath, then tiptoes away. Jude takes a labored breath, too. He's certain his precipitous life, lived at breakneck speed for nearly seven decades, is petering to a puny end. He's losing control of his thoughts, of his body. Jude follows the slip of a raindrop on the window pane until his clouded vision falls on yesterday's glass of water. Carolyn set it on the bedside table last night when she gave him his pills. Angled inside the glass is an old paper drinking straw, its red and white stripes disintegrating. She must have found it in the back of the throw-all drawer in the kitchen while looking for a plastic one.

He remembered when she tossed it in, one night in May, 1947, soon after they moved into this house, tidy and new then, their American dream built with a loan from the Veteran's Administration. That was the same night Carolyn told him with such exuberance that she was pregnant, the same night he hadn't been able to tell her he'd lost his job at Coggle Electric because he couldn't make a customer's change without his hands shaking. And Mr. Coggle had noticed. "You boys have been through a lot," Mr. Coggle said, a hand on Jude's shoulder. "But you're gonna have to get yourself straight. Use that G.I. bill. Go get you some schooling." So Jude thought about law school. He'd wanted to discuss it with Carolyn that night, but she was too excited about the baby.

He took her to the Double Do Ice Cream Shoppe where she ordered one chocolate milkshake and two red and white straws. She handed him a straw and playfully nudged the glass toward him, but he shoved it back. Two people drinking from the same cup at the same time? Someone might see, and then laugh. So she sipped it alone, gripping the fluted sides, occasionally cutting her unforgiving eyes toward him, each glance assessing one after another of his flaws. At home, she yanked open a drawer in the kitchen, threw in the unused straw she'd stuck in her purse, then slammed the drawer shut, beginning the periodic silences that became usual for them.

If Jude could go back, he'd change a lot of things. Oh, it's been decades since he has been bothered by insecurities or by hands shaking in fear of confrontation. As the attorney he eventually became, he took pride in his grand arguments of defense, his ability to assess a jury, apply the necessary words, and bring them under his sway. But now, his line of reasoning is out-of-focus. He must have slipped up somehow. But how? He had done nothing to depart from the norm.

The medicine. His confusion could be coming from the medicine they'd been giving him, some mind-changing stuff. He's heard the doctor whisper 'Alzheimer's' to Carolyn, but he knows this is a misdiagnosis: his thinking is *more* acute, not less. Incidents in his past are of critical importance now, like the straw mucking the glass of water beside him.

Carolyn creeps in again. She sees the window shade is crooked and snaps it. A surprising sound, like the long-ago smack of his father's hand.

3

"Ow! I'm sorry, Dad; I won't do it again. I won't!"

"You're only fifteen years old, Jude. A boy could get hurt in that damn billiard room!"

"I didn't want to go; David made me."

"Quit blaming your brother and own up yourself. Take responsibility!"

Carolyn sets his seven daily pills on a small tray beside the glass and notices the disintegrating straw. "I'll get some plastic ones," she says, more to herself than to him.

"I'm sorry, Carolyn," he says.

She looks at him, presses her fingers to the sides of her face like she does when she's unsure of what to do next. "Sorry for what?" she asks.

"Most all of it."

She leaves the room without comment. The glass of water on the table quivers twice with her retreating footsteps, and he is elsewhere again.

He races upstairs, his cheek stinging. He'll join the army; that's what he'll do. He'll fight for his country. America needs him, wants him, won't slap him around like that.

At dawn, he crawls out of his bedroom window onto the roof of the porch, hikes a ride with Jimmy Cage who drives a truck signed "West Alabama Dairy" and comes around each morning about that time to set two glass bottles of milk on their steps. He finishes the route with Jimmy, who is impressed that a fellow so young wants to serve, wants to "bust the butts of the Japs that killed our boys."

Jimmy gives him five bucks for good luck and promises not to tell Jude's parents he's seen him.

Jude buys a ticket on the first bus for Tuscaloosa, to enlist. He lies about his age. Camp Rucker, South Alabama, is where they send him to train. Eighty-first Division Infantry, rumored for the Pacific.

The screen door in the kitchen slams, the same sound, the same words as with every Rachel-arrival. "Morning Miss Carolyn. How's Mr. Jude?"

"Same."

"Brain pill's not helping him?" Her brown hand strokes his forehead.

"No."

"Tsk, tsk."

"Sometimes he doesn't even know me; he doesn't want to eat. Maybe we could try some oatmeal. He used to like oatmeal."

"Aw, now don't cry Miss Carolyn."

"It's time for his insulin. I guess we'll use his leg. His arm's a mess."

The island burns orange. Jude drops to the hot Pacific sand, crawls on his belly over a dismembered arm —the arm of his captain, blown to bits just as they

reached the beach. Jude is in charge now. "Run!" he yells to his men. "Jesus Christ, run!"

He doesn't recognize the two women who stand over him. The blonde one asks, "Jude, why are you yelling?" He stares blankly, trying to remember her name.

"Don't you know who I am, Jude?" she asks, the corners of her mouth stretch down to her chin as if someone has penciled a frown.

He grins. "Don't you know who you are?"

The dark-skinned woman laughs. "I reckon you've still got your sense of humor, Mr. Jude. But you know you can't run away, so quit hollerin' about it." She turns to the light-skinned one. "Maybe he needs a different kinda brain pill, Miss Carolyn."

Carolyn. Yes, her name is Carolyn. He gives a loud, guttural chuckle because he remembers.

Both women seem startled. "Uh oh," the dark face warns.

"Something's bad wrong."

Carolyn dials the bedroom phone. "Meryl, come quick. Something's wrong with your father!"

No, there isn't! Jude thinks he knows Meryl's father, and there's nothing at all wrong with him.

6

He notices the cardinal, still outside the window, and tries his humor, again. "Get away, red bird. Fly, before you're caught!"

At once, Carolyn glares at him with distaste, as an adversary might. "You were caught," she says, icily. "Years ago."

What is the woman talking about? His mind is becoming confused again, and that frightens him.

The Jap's face goes blank. His hands holding the rifle tremble. His eyes are young; they stare at Jude from a tree branch high above. In the split of a second, the Jap fires his rifle, then Jude fires at him. The young eyes squeeze shut above an opened mouth, just as a bullet slices Jude's heart. He bites through his tongue. He wets his pants. The bullet zings from his side. A Japanese child falls next to an American boy. Blood and water. Water and blood.

"Did you hear me, Jude?" the blonde woman is asking. "Meryl is here."

The one they call Meryl kisses him. "Daddy? Are you alright?"

He gives her a fine smile, but he has doubts about speaking to the blond woman again.

The father's daughter begins to cry. She turns to the blond woman. "Mom, how are you going to make it through this?"

The air medic is talking as though Jude can't hear. "I doubt he'll make it; he's shot straight through the heart."

"I'll make it" Jude gasps. "Just fly me out of this place!"

It's raining harder, but the stupid cardinal hasn't flown away; it still clings to the tree in the yard—in whose yard? He closes his eyes tightly. Whose yard? Whose house? Whose bed does he lie in? He slides a hand along the sheets and touches a memory of the blonde woman beside him. She turns her teenaged face toward his, strokes his side, whispers his name. "Jude," she calls him; "My Jude." And then, she states her warning. "Don't ever betray me, Jude Hall."

At once, it's clear. This is his house, his bed. Outside, is his yard. He is Jude Hall, a damn good lawyer. He lives in Standoff, Alabama, married to the former Carolyn Willoughby. They have a daughter, Meryl. He has all the information he needs now. It's time to get away before he's caught again.

The women have gone back into the kitchen. He can make it to the car if he's quiet. He stands up, totters a second, then moves slowly to and then through the door. If he pushes himself like he used to, he can do it. Moving faster, he makes it to the car and opens the door. The keys are in the ignition. His hands shake as he cranks it, but he turns on the wipers and backs out.

The old guy at the gas station watches as Jude drives in. "Hi'ya doin' Mr. Hall. Fill her up?"

Jude doesn't need gas, he's hungry. He tells the old man, who's squinting now, scanning the inside of Jude's car, that he wants a package of peanuts. The old guy's eyes set for a moment on Jude's pajamas, then he turns to go into the building.

"Be right back with 'em, Mr. Hall," the old guy says, his back to Jude.

Through the glass window, Jude sees him lifting the telephone. Something in his head says, "Getaway, fast!"

He flies down the highway to Tuscaloosa, to see his mama, his daddy, his brother David—to tell them he's sorry. So sorry. There's no rain here and he's smiling because he's driven for over an hour and hasn't been caught. A white frame house crowns a hill just ahead. It looks like his boyhood home. He takes the exit, pulls into the driveway.

An old woman swings on the front porch, peas in a pan on her lap. She squints, like his mother, through a patchwork of wrinkles, as if she's trying to figure out who he is. He gets out of the car, pulls up the waist of his pajamas. "I'm home!" he calls to the woman.

"Uh huh," she says, lifting a friendly, fat-knuckled hand, motioning him into the swing beside her.

He tells her what it was like back then, why he had to leave. It wasn't her; it was his father.

"Uh huh," she says, and continues to shell her peas.

He kisses her cheek, lays his head on her shoulder. "Where is my father?" he asks.

She tilts her head toward the field, toward the high corn, then rises up and retreats inside the house as if she has something urgent to do.

Jude walks to the field, approaches a tall, thin shadow that looks like his father.

His father stands within the rows, watches Jude coming, then opens his arms to fold his son in. "I knew you'd come back. I raised you tough, boy. Didn't I? I wanted to raise you tough."

Father smells like tobacco and dirt from the field, same as when Jude was a child of five, running to meet him as he came up the yard, Jude pressing his face into his father's waist, wrapping his young arms around the man he loved most in the world. Except his father shrugged him off. "Don't be such a sissy," his father said then. "Be a man!"

Maybe it's time to make amends.

Jude pulls an ear of corn, shucks it to naked, picks off the worms, bites into the kernels. It is sweet corn, but tough. He offers it to his father.

A stream of sunlight washes the field, fading the tall, thin shadow of a man to clumps of plowed earth.

Jude feels a hand on his shoulder. Two men in blue guide him back to the car, which is not his car. One of the men in blue drives that one. They drive for an hour, drive until it is raining again, then turn into a silver-soaked driveway that leads to a house he doesn't recognize.

A blonde woman waits in the bedroom, her hands pressed against her face. Another woman, with a dark face, draws back the covers. "Let's get you in bed, Mr. Jude," she says.

A third woman cries, "I'm Meryl, Daddy. Try to remember!"

He tries, *really tries* to remember. Could she be someone he loves? There's need in her voice, like the pleading of a lonely child calling for consolation, so he offers an open hand for her to come closer. At once, she steps back, as if he's pointed a finger of condemnation instead.

There's no question in his mind, now; he ought to leave again. He isn't an advocate for anyone here, and they are not advocates for him.

As soon as he can, he'll take another trip, not sure where he wants to go. All he's sure of now is that there's a boy in the corner of his mind, waiting for Jude to prove he's not guilty.

The boy has a cherub face, the face of a client Jude once defended. The boy's green eyes are still crossed, distorted by the environment that bred him. He'd taken a shotgun to his brother's head and blown it to bits, then shot his mama, shot his daddy, shot his buckshot anger into the judge's face. Jude pled with the jury, but the jury had no mercy. They condemned him. They did not see

11

the child die in their electric chair while they were home for supper. But Jude did.

The Executioner's hand is on the switch. The boy cries out, "I'm afraid, Mr. Hall. Will you hold my hand?" Their fingers entwine until the Executioner orders the bond be broken. The switch is pulled. Jude looks away. He makes the Sign of the Cross. And the boy gives up a last, brief cry of earthly pain.

"Miss Carolyn," the dark face says, peeking around the door. "Father Murray's here."

A priest comes toward him, circling purple around the shoulders of his black suit. He anoints Jude's forehead with oil and says, "In the name of the Father, and of the Son, and of the Holy Spirit."

Jude has on a wrinkled, white linen suit. He's on business in the Bahamas, is in between meetings, browsing the Straw Market with a red-headed woman from his office.

Across the street, he notices a clay-colored church. The woman is busy buying him a silly straw hat with a cardinal stuck in the band, so he leaves her to go inside. It is Saturday; there's a line for confessions. He takes his turn, pours out his infidelities of the night before.

"Bless me, Father, for I have sinned." He just wants it off his chest. He won't tell his wife. He's certain she'll never catch him.

12

"Jesus, mercy!" Jude cries abruptly, jolting the priest. His eyes switch between the man in black and the now-overturned glass of water beside the bed. He gives the priest an accusatory look that says *Why'd you spill the water on me?* His head shakes automatically. He may have wet the bed himself. So he says, "My cup runneth over," lacing the words with a smile. Even if he's losing his mind, he'll keep his sense of humor.

The blonde woman—has she always held grudges?—calls out, "Rachel, come here. Mr. Jude needs a change."

The priest leaves. The father's daughter puts an arm around the blonde woman. The dark-skinned one throws back his covers, exposing all Jude tried to keep secret.

"Oh come on, Jude; let's see what you've got." The red-headed woman grabs at his fly, unzips his trousers.

He moves away to call Carolyn. He'll be late tonight, he tells her. He has a deposition to work on, but after that he'll be home. She hangs up without saying a word.

He recalls the picture he has on his desk at the office, of himself with his wife. She is looking at him. She knows what he's doing in the Bahamas. She knows what he'll keep doing when he gets home.

The dark-skinned one pulls the covers back over him. She wads up the stained plastic and paper, then stuffs it in the trash. "You're all done, now," she says as Jude turns toward the window. "What are you looking at Mr. Jude—that straw hat with the red bird stuck on it? I'll get it for you when it stops raining so hard."

The father's daughter touches his cheek as if she has to explain. "You brought the hat home years ago, from the Bahamas, and gave it to Mama." She turns to the blonde woman, "Tell him about it, Mama. It might help him remember."

The woman doesn't respond. Jude doesn't expect her to. Her thoughts are reflected in the water glass beside him, swirling from white, to red, to an indescribable murk, while his own thoughts are suddenly lucid. Even then he'd tried for humor when he realized Carolyn knew.

Jude awoke in a bed,
a white hat on his head,
with a woman, called Red
And soon he'll be dead.

She hadn't laughed, had let him hear nothing but his own gross, forced chuckle.

She snatches the hat from his hands. He hadn't seen it for years, until his diabetes worsened, and his mind muddled more and more, and his bedroom became his only court room. A few days ago she produced it as evidence in her case against him. Then she stormed out and tied it to the tree just outside their bedroom window, hurrying back inside to tell him that now he'd never be able to get away from what he'd done to her.

The blonde woman glances out of the window, at the hat with the cardinal, twisting in the beating rain. The father's daughter consoles the blonde woman when she

14

starts to cry. Then they go out of the room. The dark-skinned one stabs his arm with another measure of insulin. "One more shot of this good stuff, Mr. Jude, before I leave for the night." She tosses the used needle in a yellow trash basket, then gives him a pill to sleep. "Sweet dreams."

The man in the wrinkled linen suit takes off his white straw hat and slings it on the bedpost, evaluating Jude with his eyes. Jude tries to shrink to nothing and wake up, as usual. But this time, he senses that the man will not be outsmarted. Then a smile crinkles the old man's face.

Jude recognizes him immediately. He's seen him in the mirror for years, weighing his every defense. "How'd I come out?" Jude asks.

The old guy smiles as if he's known the ending all along. "You soaked yourself, son, but I never gave up on you. Are you ready to leave it behind?"

An hour before dawn, Jude swallows a deep, sudden breath with which he leaves behind all that ties him.

The sun is shining when Carolyn finds him that morning, and kneels beside the bed to pray for his soul. But she does not bend forward to kiss lips that lied to her. She does not reach out to hold hands that held someone else.

When she hears Rachel arrive, Carolyn calls for her to come into the bedroom. "Lord, lord," Rachel says when she sees Jude. "He still got a smile on his face!" Then she covers the smile with the bed sheet. "Better go call the funeral home."

"Call Meryl first," Carolyn says, still on her knees.

Meryl comes quickly enough to see two funeral home attendants carrying Jude out on a stretcher. She gives a sharp cry.

"Let her see him one last time," one attendant says to the other, and they let down the legs on the stretcher, just under the arthritic tree. The straw hat makes a dark, green shadow on the sheet covering her father. Meryl looks up to see that the washed-out, red cardinal still hangs to its brim.

An attendant folds back the sheet, and Meryl kisses her father's lips and strokes his hands, one crossed over the other. Then she goes inside to comfort her mother. An hour later, they back out of the driveway for the funeral home to make preparations.

"Want me to get rid of that old red bird while you're gone?" Rachel calls out.

Carolyn shakes her head emphatically, no.

•

During the night, Carolyn, dreams her own recurring dream, the one where she is confronted by Jude in a wrinkled linen suit and a white panama hat. He begs her forgiveness, as he has for years.

In the morning she runs her finger across the cardinal. If ever, it will be some time before she unfastens the red bird and lets it go.

Dragon

I keep my head down when I sign for a Gulf front room, not wanting to face the night clerk. She directs me to the fifth floor: shell-shaped pillows on a king-sized bed, gauzy drapery mimicking crystal green water, and double-paned windows, framing a fire-breathing, dragon-like sunset.

At home, in Highlow, they'd quoted St. Cyril.

"Beware of the dragon," they'd said about Richard.

I stretch out on the king-sized bed and turn on the massage. The pulsing reminds me of his fingers and the expensive bottle of sun block he bought, all of which he used on me. Richard liked manipulation, the slip-sliding feel of possession. Maybe he was born that way and couldn't help it. Maybe I could have changed him. Then maybe he wouldn't have died.

•

For months, I was Richard's only nurse; the one he'd been having an affair with was afraid to touch him after she learned he had AIDS. He didn't cheat anymore, and he didn't lie, except in the bed he'd made for himself.

At home I was taught compassion, so I timed out medication every four hours, kept watch that the oxygen hose stayed in his nostrils, that the battery worked in case of a storm surge; but I resented the stench of his bed pan, the ooze of his lesions, the diapers wrapped around hips so thin that bones showed through tissue-paper skin. The man betrayed me after all.

"Don't' trust him," they'd said.

Before I left Mobile, I telephoned Anthony, Richard's best friend, to say I was leaving. Again, Anthony said, "I love you." He wanted to know if I loved him. I gave no answer.

"I think you do love me." An empty pause and then, "Richard's death was an accident, Liz. You didn't create the storm. I'll call your cell tomorrow."

·

A ruthless streak of sunlight wakes me. Beyond the paned window the sand is sugar, the Gulf opals. A patch of blue sky births an unblemished sun, so holy in appearance I turn away.

I leave behind my cell phone. I want no communication. I take the elevator, going over lies I might tell my family as to why I'm coming home. On the beach, I realize how hard it will be to fool them.

"He won't bring out your best," they'd said.

Once, we built a castle here, Richard and I, with delicate turrets of dribbled water thinly mixed with sand.

In my palm, the water looked pink and blue, the colors of dreams. I imagined we lived inside, until a wave exploded, and thousands of tiny, silver mirrors turned it back to common sand.

"Let's build another." But Richard walked away.

"Unreliable," they'd said.

A small crab creeps out of a nearby hole. It peeps up with black dot eyes that judge me, then scuttles sideways across the whiteness, leaving a sketchy trail.

Overhead glides a V-shape of sea gulls, an arrow pointing north. A little girl emerges from behind a dune of sea oats. The beach-child's eyes are bright with marvel. She runs beneath the sailing birds, as if their magical wings are all she ever wanted, as if they might swoop down and carry her away to enchantment.

A bikini-clad woman and a fat-bellied man follow, the man clutching an over-sized Solo cup. He hurls a hairy arm at the gulls. "Here come the shit-bombers!" He pretends to safeguard the woman by tossing a beach towel over her head.

She throws off the towel. "Quit it!" she days, but warns the child, "Look out them birds don't dump on you, Shugah."

The child looks up, grabs the woman's hand, and the three of them break into a run down the beach, away from the fairy-tale.

"He's not the prince you think he is."

A lone man, pale, bald, and heavy with middle-age, trudges in my direction. He's fair-skinned, like me at risk for a burn. Already, the sun has blistered the crown of his head. He has a dog on a leash, one of those little ones with the big barks. The man yanks on the leash when the little dog barks at the waves, but it continues to bark, and the man continues to yank. Finally, the dog bites the man on his leg. The man doesn't appear angry that his pet turned on him. He gives the dog a forgiving pat, like he'll love him no matter what, and they continue down the beach.

"You'll spend your life forgiving him."

The woman, man, and child, come back up the beach. The child whines, "I wanna 'Co-cola,'" then cries that she's hot and tired and no one will carry her. Neither the man nor the woman picks her up.

"Gotta get home on your own, Baby Doll," the woman says, wiping sweat off her face. "Hurry up. Looks like a storm."

Back in the room, my cell phone rings. From the balcony, a dark cloud covers the sun. Bronzed bodies scramble, hide beneath weak-roofed pavilions, rocking in a storm to be wary of. Lightening smears the sky; thunder cracks wildly, same as the night Richard died.

•

It was storming when Anthony came. He and Richard talked about their long friendship, about their mutual work as physicians, about Anthony finding a

20

woman to settle down with. When Richard's voice became too weak, Anthony said he ought to rest, then followed me to the other bedroom. It was only sex; my payback to Richard—because he was not a prince, and I wouldn't spend my life forgiving him.

In darkness, I unmade the bed, not realizing the power had been off so long and the battery for Richard's oxygen had run down, shutting off the flow. I gave Anthony what he wanted, and found some sense of vindication. In the other room, Richard gasped for air, and found none.

•

Around noon, I leave Gulf Shores and take I-10 across the Florida Panhandle, still wondering how I'll explain why I've come home. At Pensacola, the bridge over Escambia Bay is under construction from a recent hurricane, so I inch along with a convoy of others on a two-lane county road, all the way around the bay, to get to some useable interstate.

In the tiny town of Vigil, nearly out of gas, I leave the procession to fill up at a run-down station buttressed by a rusty-roofed café. But when I try to get back in line, no one will give up space to let me in, so I back up the BMW and go inside the café for a cup of coffee, thinking a little time might produce a Good Samaritan on the road.

The inside is crammed with three Formica-topped tables. The two in front are taken by men in work

21

clothes speaking Spanish. The third table is empty. It's in the back corner next to a closed door that likely leads to the kitchen. I take that one and sit down to the company of a napkin dispenser and a clay pot holding a Christmas cactus with four pink buds, just forming.

An old, black waitress in a starched white uniform— she must weigh three hundred pounds—leaves the men and comes to hand me a one-page, plasticized menu. "Sweet tea, Hon?"

I want coffee, but not words, so I nod yes for the tea and take the menu, except I don't look at it. I look at the cactus. Richard once gave me a cactus just like it. I thought it would require no care. Not so. It needed water, fertilization two or three times a week, and pruning. It was a delicate plant that required a watchful eye. It died during the first November we were married.

"The barbecue's real good. You want a barbecue sammich?" the waitress asks.

I shake my head, no, just as the blast of a radio comes behind me: *"Hey you ho, you bitchin' ho; why you try to kill me with yo stankin mojo?"*

The waitress twists toward the kitchen. "Cut that stuff off, Cecil!"

"Aw Grandmaw!" But the radio stops.

The waitress shakes her head in dismay. "Lord, Jesus," she whispers, reaching over me to poke her thumb into the soil of the cactus, as if checking for moisture. I catch the crisp smell of her starched white uniform.

"Honey, whatever happened to sweet Aretha?" she asks, like she's known both the singer and me all our lives. "Can't nobody spell R-E-S-P-E-C-T, anymore? I love that boy, but I told him and told him; 'Cecil, that music you always playin' is a recipe for ruin!' He puts his hands over his ears whenever I say it, but he hears me. He ain't a bad boy, he just don't use his brains sometimes. You know how kids are nowadays."

She waits for me to respond. Instead, my eyes fill.

"What's wrong, Baby?" The waitress takes a napkin from the dispenser and hands it to me.

I can't even say *thank you*.

"Well, I'm gonna get that barbeque sammich. It'll make you feel better, and the pork's real fresh." She touches my shoulder as she leaves the table, like she cares. She wouldn't bother if she really knew me.

She comes back with the tea, and the sandwich is huge. A pickle on top, chips piled round it. She smiles, watching me take a bite. "That's some good ole soul food, ain't it, Hon?"

I glance up and smile, only an attempt to return her kindness. She drops heavily into the opposite chair and reaches for my hand. Her eyes pin me, appear to see right through me. She reins me so close I can't pull back without being rude. The tender buds on the table quiver and the fork clinks against the plastic tea glass. "You need some comfort, doncha Shug? Well, I'm ready to listen. "

But I can't handle her now! An image in my mind, when I found Richard dead, is scaring the hell out of me.

"Oh, go on now; you know you need to. Like I told Cecil; I ain't gonna judge you." Then she laughs. "Takes somebody even bigger than me to do that."

"We go to the Father of Souls," they'd said.

In the end, I revealed to the waitress what I meant to hide. She couldn't have thought much of me afterward. I had a little breakdown, and I didn't eat the sandwich. I told her about St. Cyril and the dragon, about Richard and Anthony. She called for Cecil to take it to the kitchen and wrap it up for me.

Then she grasped my hand. "Listen Shugah, we all got to pass by the dragon. That fire-breathing sucker's gonna be there, waiting with his jaws open 'cause he's gotta be fed. Don't give him nothing else to eat. Go on home and tell 'em the truth."

Cecil came back with the gold-foiled package and a thick paper napkin. He handed it to the waitress, who handed it to me. I took it to be nice, I wasn't a bit hungry. Talking about truth usually tempers my appetite.

Minutes later, back in the red BMW, I wait nearly twenty more minutes for a space in the traffic. A young girl with long brown hair finally lets me in, but she isn't a Good Samaritan; she's dropped her cell phone and has to brake a few seconds to reach for it, so I T-bone in front of her.

The sandwich, a bit of the sauce escaping, is captured in foil beside me, blinking like a yellow gold caution light on the sunlit seat. Fifty miles from Highlow, I'm hungry, and tear into it; consume every chunk of it, until

I'm holding only the crushed gold wrapper as if it's part of the steering wheel.

I notice barbecue sauce, thick as blood, on my hands. I wipe it away with the napkin, stuff the trash into the litter bag on the floor of the BMW and take the next exit home. But I don't intend to tell anything close to the truth as the waitress suggested. I'll lie, as I always do when I'm trapped in the jaws of something I've done.

•

When I found Richard dead, the mirror reflected a fearful creature, crouching above his body as if to devour it. I had to look twice; it took me a long time to see the dragon. It took me a long time to see that the reflection was . . . me.

Shooting at Heaven's Gate

I.

Satan is crouching at your door! You ain't seen him coming, boy. Nobody seen him coming but the Lord Jesus Christ. Now, he's after you. Don't wait for his spear. Conquer him!

On the last day of the Spring term, Edmund had to leave the teacher's podium during a Sociology class because his grandfather's fanatical voice would not depart from his head.

Standing in front of his class, he couldn't remember the point he was making and his teacher voice began to tremble; so he lifted the sheet of notes he'd made as a reminder, but the notes seemed to will themselves into a crumpled ball then fly from his hand toward the back of the room. His students looked stunned. Several dodged the paper ball, and the rest turned their eyes downward, as if they were embarrassed for him, as if he didn't measure up to their expectations, and never would.

He felt nauseated, mumbled some excuse, left the class room and headed down the hall to the men's room, just as the squatty shadow of Mal Hawkins emerged from its fluorescent glare. And therein lies your ruin, Edmund. *I've told you to nip him in the bud. But will you listen? No!*

"You all right?" Mal asked, holding open the door for Edmund to enter. "

"Fine!" he snapped at the psychology professor, while in his mind his grandfather went on and on about the fact that Edmund was not fine. Not fine at all.

"See you tonight then." Mal said. "We'll get you feeling better—that is, if your wife will let you out."

"Oh, she'll let me out alright," Edmund said. "She doesn't tell me what to do."

Mal grinned as he left, and the door to the men's room swung closed behind him.

Are you afraid change will be painful? Let me tell you, Edmund, it will be painful. It will hurt like fiery Hell, but it sure beats going there! Edmund looked at his face in the bathroom mirror, deep into his eyes for signs of inherited lunacy. He needed help from Mal, and the psychologist never failed to offer it.

That night, he told Ginnie he was going for a run, but he went to Mal's house, instead—for instruction on how to silence his grandfather's voice, once and for all— and for the cocaine. Except this time, Dr. Mal's prescription was different. He offered him marijuana, setting a plate full of joints on the glass coffee table between them as Ginnie might set out a snack of crackers and cheese. Mal didn't take a joint; he never did. Edmund smoked two or three as he unburdened himself with recitations of his grandfather's rants, while Mal sat across from him in a plush velvet chair, sniffing, or frowning, or raising his chin disapprovingly. Then, looking bored, the psychologist got up in the middle of

Edmund's soliloquy, went to his desk, and opened a drawer.

Edmund stopped talking at once, hoping to see Mal take out some cocaine. He'd never buy it himself, but if Mal offered it, he wouldn't refuse. When Mal turned to face him with a gun in his hand, Edmund jerked backward.

Mal looked amused, his clay-colored skin hanging on the sharp bones of his face like peanut butter spread over a pine cone—Ginnie's bait to lure hungry birds into their yard. He tossed the gun into Edmund's lap and sat across from him again. "It's only to remind the voice in your head to leave you alone. Now, you're in control, just like the old man says you should be."

Edmund fingered the revolver. He'd always been fascinated by guns. This one was a Bersa Thunder .380 with an exposed hammer, steel slide and an aluminum alloy frame. It felt good in his hands. He looked over at Mal and saw that he was smiling.

"Your grandfather is dead," Mal said, "and—I should hardly have to say this, because we both know it damn well—the god he talked about was never alive. It was you who invented their rants, so it's you who must get rid of the voices. The gun is only a symbol to remind you of that." Then he tapped his fingers on the arm of the chair, waiting for a response.

He supposed it was simple, what Mal said, even reasonable. "Maybe he is dead," Edmund agreed, not sure whether he meant God or his grandfather.

Mal stood up quickly. "Maybe is not the right answer." He snatched the gun from Edmund's hands, tossed it back into the drawer, then nodded toward the six joints still on the table. "Take a few of those home with you. I'm not sure I can help you tonight." Then tilting his head to meet Edmund's gaze, he said, "Maybe next time."

Next time? If Ginnie had anything to do with it, there wouldn't be one. She'd always disliked Mal, but her spite was increased a few weeks later when she and Edmund attended a cocktail party for faculty members at his house. An End of Summer party, Mal called it.

Edmund noticed that the psychologist seemed to find Ginnie the most desirable person there, when she surely was not. She'd had an outbreak of acne and gained at least ten pounds over the summer, so Edmund was surprised to see Mal's dark eyes flit toward Ginnie each time she spoke, or laughed, or tugged at her too-tight dress.

Ginnie didn't seem aware of it though; her habit was never to pay Mal any attention. But late in the evening, after she'd had several glasses of wine, she made a giddy announcement that came as surprise to Edmund. "Everyone, gather round," she said. "I want to tell you about my good fortune."

Mal's guests stopped talking and turned their attention to Ginnie, who was slyly smiling, and now, looking pointedly at Mal. "I've developed a new course for my Fall English classes," she said. "It's called The

Voice of God in Literature, and it has already been approved by the Dean!"

At once, Mal's covetous eyes ceased to flutter. Other members of the faculty flocked around Ginnie, chirping cheerfully about her course, but Mal set his drink down hard on the glass table and abruptly left the room—his usual sign that a visit, or a party, was over. Ginnie didn't seem the least concerned by his exit and, for at least another hour, kept the group engrossed in the specifics of her new course.

On the following morning, Mal called the Dean at home to protest the legality of such a course for a public college. When the Dean, who happened to be Ginnie's mother's first cousin, sloughed him off, Mal took it to the Board of Directors, insisting on the likely loss of government funding. Two board members pecked away at Ginnie's course until it died a bloody death.

When Ginnie learned of it she was furious. At first, Edmund thought her anger was aimed at him. He breathed a sigh of relief when she said, "I'll be damned if I'll let Mal Hawkins crucify my course!" Then piece by piece, he began to pick up the too-tight clothes she was throwing all around the bedroom, and took her side. "You're resourceful. You'll come up with something."

Ginnie applied her forte, a razor-sharp ability to uncover a person's defects. She made a visit to each of the two board members who'd impaled her course, pointing out her knowledge about a few of their seamy flaws, and making it clear that those imperfections would be extremely interesting to her cousin, the Dean. By afternoon, her course had been rescheduled.

Mal, whose ears were everywhere in the community college's halls, quickly learned about the reinstatement, and made an angry telephone call to Edmund. "Why didn't you stop her? Whose side are you on?"

"I'm not taking sides."

"Lukewarm, huh?" Mal scoffed. "Look, let me tell you one thing. I happen to know that even your grandfather's so-called god doesn't tolerate lukewarms. Better hope he doesn't spit you out of his mouth!" He said it like it would be a while before the door of his house would be open to Edmund.

Edmund sat on the bed's edge. This morning, a week before the beginning of the Fall term. Ginnnie was dressing in a pair of over-washed, baggy red pants, the same color, and with about as much shape, as an old, sun-bleached tractor Edmund's grandfather left for years —simply dead, in the middle of a field. She put them on as a kind of flag claiming the few days left before each of them would rise and dress as Bethel Community College again. "I like to take advantage of these remaining summer days," she told him.

But what she likes more is to be ornery. She knows very well he hates it when she dresses like that. What she really meant to do when she put on the discolored pants, the stained T-shirt imprinted with Roll Tide, when she left off her make-up and balled her hair on the top of

32

her head, was to drive a nail into his pride, quashing any remaining thoughts that she might try to please him.

He, of course, is always professional. Summer or not, when he goes to any public place, he wears a suit and tie, same as he wears to teach his Sociology courses. His body is as fit as his mind. He maintains a gym habit, eats the right food; all the things that Ginnie lets slide. "It's showing on you," he told her this morning, knowing that this would be his first shot in one more tiresome battle between them.

Looking at her in the faded pants, he thought about her frequent appointments with the dermatologist, and how, after each visit to Dr. Burke, she went on and on about what a marvelous doctor he was. Jealously overwhelmed him, and so he said, "It surprises the hell out of me that even a one-legged skin doctor would find you attractive enough for an affair." He said it as if he had proof, which he didn't; and as if he didn't love her, which he did.

She turned an offended face toward him. At first, she was methodical, nearly meek in her response. She said she empathized with her dermatologist because he'd lost a leg in Afghanistan, lost it fighting bravely for his country. "But I've never, ever, thought of Dr. Burke in a sexual way." Then all at once her eyes narrowed. She swiped a hand through the air and suspended it above the crown of his head. Her fingers curled as if they held a gun. "I know who put that garbage into your mind—Mal Hawkins, the foulest man I know!"

He shoved her hand away. "Not true," he said, and felt at once as though split in half. He knew the Psychology professor before he knew Ginnie and had found his friendship beneficial, and, at times, even necessary.

"It is true!" She stomped to the bedroom dresser, and snatched up their wedding photo: Ginnie, slim and beautiful then, in a wedding dress, her loving eyes set on Edmund; and Edmund, in his tuxedo of black and white, his eyes aimed away from Ginnie toward the silver border around the periphery of the photo, as if someone more important had just summoned his attention. He recalled that the 'someone' had been Mal Hawkins, his best man.

She tossed the photograph on the bed beside him. "He's always been the problem between us, you just won't admit it. Mal Hawkins masquerades as a sweet little songbird, ever ready to sing to you—or bring you anything you want. But—and there aren't many folks you can say this about directly, he's a flat-out false friend and anything you accept from him will kill you, Edmund." She was behind him then; he imagined the scornful look on her face as she ranted on and on. "My God, the man needs to be in an asylum, not teaching at the college. Even on his deathbed, and I don't claim to know exactly why, but your grandfather tried to warn you about him."

The old man was still trying to warn him when he awoke this morning while Ginnie, a silhouette in the early light, was tightly shrouded in a sheet on her side of the bed. You know where that bird's carrying you, don't you, Edmund? To the thorn of impalement. Take charge. Change your ways. Now! More old and tiring words from the grave.

But Ginnie's flesh-and-blood words were no better. Her attempt to manipulate his every move aggravated Edmund equally as much as the preacher voice in his head. To prove to her that manipulation didn't work with him, and that he meant to act and think as he wanted, Edmund visited Mal once a week—or more, if the psychologist invited him. But Ginnie had never allowed Mal in their house, and after the debacle over her new course, Edmund knew Mal meant what he said when he banned him from further visits.

Except, except with Mal bans and the lifting of bans was business as usual. Last night, Mal had called. "I have to say, miss our conversations, Edmund. I don't think we ought to let your overly assertive wife push either one of us around, do you? So why don't you just come on over tomorrow evening?"

He heard resentment in the way Mal referred to Ginnie, and he'd always realized that for some reason Mal seemed determined to sway Edmund's opinion of her. But the first thing he'd thought of when he heard Mal's voice was drugs, not Ginnie; and the second thing was that either cocaine or marijuana would do. Edmund was anxious to go.

He hadn't been inside the house five minutes when Mal asked, "Do you think Ginnie is having an affair with her dermatologist?"

Edmund looked around the table for a joint, though cocaine was what he really wanted. "I'm not sure. Sometimes I could shoot her for what she does." It was an off-handed statement; he'd just remembered the gun in Mal's desk drawer.

Mal gave a quick smile, as though Edmund had at last taken a right direction. "I'll be just a minute." He left the room, and when he returned, he laid a gun on the glass-topped table, and spread out a few heaping lines of cocaine. Then he stood back, as if he'd just fed a hungry dog from which he'd intentionally withheld food, so he could get a grateful wag of its tail.

Edmund didn't want to be grateful to him. He didn't want to convey to anyone else that they might have hold of his collar. Ginnie and his grandfather were enough to contend with. So, he tried not to appear too pleased with Mal's offering, nudging the conversation away from Ginnie and her dermatologist, back to the subject of his grandfather. "I need to get rid of the old man's voice," he said, looking up at Mal. For years, he'd longed to silence his grandfather's voice, but the old man's warnings had only become more frequent. And now, increasingly urgent. And after all, Mal was accomplished. He was President of the Alabama Regional Association of Psychologists, and his name was attached to several research papers. Edmund hadn't read any of them, though he'd been meaning to read the most recent one, "The True Meaning of Good and Evil."

"Tell me about your grandfather, Mal said.

He thought he'd already told him enough over the years, but he took some cocaine and began to repeat it. "The man who raised me—a Holiness preacher—was a holy tyrant, a tall, hungry-looking figure with a prophet's unkempt beard, who constantly cornered me, demanding that I justify even the smallest endeavor. First he would ask me, 'What is its nature,' Edmund? And next, 'Is it sinful?' But before I could offer an opinion, he'd caution, 'Think carefully now. A mistake could cost you eternal life.' Sometimes the grilling took hours because he wouldn't let up until I gave him the answer he wanted. Then he'd pat me on the back and say, 'Only the holy are happy.'" Edmund didn't say so to Mal, but, oddly, revisiting those days, he felt a measure of satisfaction, even certainty, that he and his grandfather were pursuing genuine Truth. After he earned his doctorate, though, and became a professor—and especially, after he met Mal—he lost any gratification he'd found in coming up with correct answers, be it to please his grandfather or his grandfather's god. Within a few years he'd traded this gratification for the sheer delight that came from, almost always with Mal, deriding the old man and his message.

"What do you think your grandfather wants you to do?"

"The thing he said most was, 'Fix yourself, boy, lest you miss the promise of something grand.'" Edmund ran an impatient finger through the drug on the table.

"Well, you could take his advice; be open to doing something grand, and solve the problem of Ginnie, too. You know, kill two birds with one stone?" Mal paused, as if waiting for a response, but Edmund was considering that 'something off-balanced' was occurring.

"Are you listening?" Mal's voice was stern. "There is one easy measure that could produce something grand, just one easy measure with Ginnie."

"Oh?" he responded, his eyes coveting the white crack until he could wait no longer for more. He reached for another chip, and put the shooter to his lips. "What easy measure is that?"

Mal leaned back on plush, red cushions and cocked his head in another assessment. "An act of masculine ferocity would be to your advantage. You've heard of the old wives' tale of scaring a person to stop his hiccups? Just frighten her a little. Besides, that grandness you talk of? It's there. It's just repressed. You need to let it out."

"How?"

"I'll loan you the gun. As long as you—be careful to cover yourself. Don't you dare mention my name. Don't you dare. This is between you and your grandfather and your wife, alright?"

The psychologist rose to re-open his desk drawer. His clay-colored skin skulked down the sharp bones of his face as he found the revolver and offered it to Edmund once more. "Come on, Edmund, we've talked countless times about avoiding the old professor's trap—the inability to take action. Won't it be grand to take charge?"

"Yes, grand, but—"

"Just put the gun in your pocket!"

He did as Mal ordered, then went back to the cocaine. While he was snorting some, Mal said offhandedly. "By the way, did you hear that Ginnie's dermatologist, who, I'm sure you know, is married to Eleanor in the English Department, is getting a divorce from his wife? He must have a girlfriend somewhere."

II.

The noise comes at the tail-end of their argument, a detonation from somewhere outside of himself, a loud and vulgar vibration like the violent burst of a worn-out tire from the nearby four-lane highway that crosses the town of Bethel. And afterward, Ginnie is finally quiet and still. Her head rests against the back of the orange, second hand sofa, one leg extended, the other tucked beneath her. Her sky-blue eyes are turned coldly toward him, waiting for him to say he's sorry.

He wants to give her an apology, but anything he says to her now, will go unheard.

Except he is sorry, maybe even the "sorriest person in the state of Alabama." Just before the noise, she flung those words at him, along with her wedding ring. He'd been trying to open the front door to get away from her list of condemnations—that Mal was taking over him, that the drugs were warping his mind, that his jealousy of Dr. Burke was out of control. But his hands were too sweaty to turn the brass knob. The air conditioner wasn't working; it was as if the house and Ginnie intended to smother him on account of his deficiencies.

So he'd turned toward her; yanked off his wedding ring, too, then tossed it on the floor next to hers and stomped them both.

"So what if Mal gives me a few drugs—you know the kind of headaches I have!" He was inches away, pointing a finger in her face. "Who do you think you are for putting me down? I could have had any woman I wanted; I didn't have to pick you. I'm not jealous of a one-legged skin doctor, and I am not out of control!"

He said all that to her, and more—before the noise.

But now, fingers of sunlight steal through the slatted shutters behind the sofa, slip across her face, caressing her cheeks, touching her mouth, as if kissing her. He remembers how sweet it is to kiss her and he wants to, but her lips are closed to him. He's glad her lips are closed; she can't call him "a lunatic" again.

She used to call him "wonderful, baby" and "the answer to my prayers." She used to stroke his face and look at him as if he were a splendid gift. Today, she'd said there was foulness inside him. She said she wouldn't make love to him anymore, until what he loved most was her.

He extends a palm toward the sofa where Ginnie is sprawled; a conciliatory gesture, but she doesn't appear to notice, so he slams the end table with his fist and three framed pictures wobble out of place. He returns them to proper order.

The first picture was taken by his father on the day of his Baptism. In it, he is wrapped in a lacy white garment in the arms of his mother. Her long, dark hair falls over

40

the crown of his head. A few streaks of gray reveal that he was her surprise baby, her only child when she thought she'd never have one. She wanted him to be like her, to be a teacher. Staring at the picture, he can see how terribly she loved him.

The second picture is of his First Communion. He is meticulously dressed in a blue blazer and red-striped tie, standing in the center of the last row because he's the tallest child in the class. His face, his fingernails, and his innocent hands are clean. He is smiling at his father, who is taking the picture, and at his mother, because she's dabbing her eyes with a Kleenex. Just behind him is the kind priest, and beyond the priest is courageous Jesus on the wood of the Cross, which is hung on a wooden wall. Afterward, they will go to the Church Hall for orange juice in paper cups, and bacon and eggs and sweet rolls. He will sit between his lovely mother, a grateful convert, and his father, a firm Catholic. Beside his place at the table, safe from stains of bacon grease, he will lay the missal the kind priest has given him, with its mother-of-pearl cover impressed with a gold chalice. Inside the front cover, are hand-written words: "God loves you, Eddie. He will love you despite what you do, because God never changes."

The last picture, taken by his mother, is of his father standing behind what was left of the full-flowered dogwood tree his mother planted in their backyard when she and his father built the house. The dogwood lies horizontally on the ground. His father, in a red plaid shirt, has just cut it down because it became diseased. Minutes after she took the picture, his mother had cut a

41

vase-worth of branches with white-petaled flowers, centered with crowns. She poured some water in the old heirloom vase and handed them to him. "Edmund"—she never called him Eddie, as the priest did—"put these on the dining room table." It was Good Friday and his grandparents were coming for Easter Sunday. The old man, a Holiness preacher, was a warrior for Jesus Christ, always out to get Edmund.

Now, Ginnie is out to get him, too.

He needs air. He needs to get away from Ginnie's scrutinizing banter. Her spite has re-triggered his chronic headaches. They grip like a vise around his ears, behind his eyes, down the bridge of his nose until he can barely breathe. He tries the front door again, strengthening his grip on the door knob. At last, it opens to a withered yard of dead grass where a lone Loggerhead Shrike picks through the dry dirt with its hooked beak, chasing after a brown lizard. It flies away when he hustles down the walkway toward the curb and his car.

He notices the pines on the other side of the street are an odd, night-colored green. They seem pasted to the sky. Two elongated contrails of airplanes from the nearby airport converge above the pines in an X which, when he looks again, assumes the shape of a cross. He recalls the wooden cross on the wooden wall in the church of his childhood. He recalls the inscription the priest wrote in his First Communion missal: "God loves you, Eddie. He will love you despite what you do, because God never changes." Then the pale yellow lines fragment and distort into lips, opening like a mouth, and he hears his name, Edmund, as if he's being called to repent for what he's just done.

He yanks open the car door and gets in. It was only an X. Not a cross. Grandfather—get away! But the humming of the car's air-conditioner reminds him of the stirring of fans in the holiness pedlar's church. He sees himself in the pew, slipping away, little by little, from the old preacher's words in the pulpit. "Oh, you've done it, Edmund. You've done it, now! Beg for forgiveness. Change yourself, or you'll never climb the ladder to eternal life."

Beside him on the seat is a neat stack of jackets, several sweaters, and the winter face mask he used for deer hunting. Ginnie gathered them up yesterday and told him to take the stuff to the Bethel Rescue Mission. He studies the face mask, thinking she's trying to do it again, trying to control me again, masking her disapproval of hunting with a good deed. His hand closes into another fist. He won't give up hunting! He shoves the stack of clothes to the floor board, slams the accelerator, and skids off.

The tires of his car squeal like the wild hog he once shot as a boy on his grandfather's land. They'd been after deer, but the old man determined from the rounded tracks around his deer feed that hogs were eating the corn instead, and he meant to get rid of them. They'd waited in the deer blind for hours until a hog came. "You take that devil down," he whispered to Edmund. "And don't flinch and foul it up." He hadn't flinched. He hadn't fouled it up—then.

43

Now, the squeal of the hog, like his grandfather's voice, resurrects in his head. He tries to block out the sounds, but a whirring takes over, louder and louder, like the vulgar detonation he heard this morning, and then, like sirens warning the town. He turns right, and then left, with no thought as to where he's going. He just wants to get rid of the whining in his head. He reminds himself that he's his own man, that he's in charge, and that he'll allow no one to do him wrong. Oh, they'll try; he knows they will. And who are 'they'? Well, he's made a numbered list in his mind. Dr. Burke, Ginnie's divorced dermatologist, is the first one on it.

He passes the Rescue Mission but doesn't remember the clothes, and then Hubble Hardware, Radio Shack, Pretty Pearl's Beauty Parlor, and Gunter's Guns—all in one large brick building erected as a hotel in 1820 when the town was founded as a port-of-call for steamboats on the Chattahoochee. Back then, Bethel was booming with success. "Heaven's Gate," the old riverboat captains called it, as though heaven's portal had come down to earth. Until the railroads came and Heaven's Gate declined. Then the town became Bethel again.

But his grandfather had liked the old name, the biblical Bethel, where Jacob dreamed of a ladder ascending to heaven. Over the years, it had been the subject of many of his sermons. Edmund remembered one in particular he'd heard as a boy. The week before his grandfather preached it, he'd nearly killed a schoolmate with his fists. All he recalls about the beating now is that the kid tried to take something from his desk, something that belonged to Edmund. "Thou shalt not covet!" Edmund had hollered with every blow.

During the sermon, his grandfather pointed a finger, stiff as a gun, toward his entire congregation, but Edmund knew the old man aimed only at him. Do you think you're at Heaven's Gate? Do you think you can climb the ladder? Well, you'll never climb it unless you're pure as fallen snow. Unless you leave room for God's wrath, not your own. Repent!

He takes another left and passes the place where his grandfather's old Holiness Church once stood. Now the sign reads: Dermatology Clinic. He pictures the one-legged Dr. Burke inside, coveting Ginnie. Maybe he's deciding how to position her on his examination table the next time she begs him to fix her acne-pocked face. Maybe he'll set his doctor's eyes and mouth inches from hers, and try to take what doesn't belong to him, while Ginnie smiles with misdirected sympathy. Then he pictures Ginnie at home, probably still quiet on the couch, counting the hours until her next appointment with the doctor.

Damn Ginnie. Damn the doctor. He means to teach them both a lesson for messing with what belongs to him! He listens for his grandfather's voice, and hears nothing—except the bothersome squeals of the hog. He sees himself standing over it as it quivers and dies, recalling the pride he felt in killing it because the varmint wanted what wasn't his.

After that, he's unaware of anything he passes, even unaware of his own thoughts, as if he is the automobile, a changeless, mechanized vehicle set on auto-pilot, incapable of turning around on its own. It's a disposition he developed as a ten-year-old child during the accident in which his parents were killed by a drunk driver. Edmund emerged unscathed, with only his chronic headaches, from a head injury he caused himself by beating his forehead against a piece of twisted steel—all that was left of the front seat where the distorted, dead bodies of his mother and father were entrapped, then pried out, and taken away. The doctors said the head injury probably didn't alter his brain, but he knows it did. Sometimes he feels he's still in the car with them, still beating his head; the way he feels during his headaches, the way he feels right now, and he wallows in it. Why did it have to be him? Why did it have to be his parents? He's angry, so angry he could bust up the world. Again, he recalls the boy at school, crying as he hit him; the thieving hog, quivering as he killed it. And Ginnie, finally quiet, after calling him an incurable, drug-addicted lunatic.

Unexpectedly, he finds himself on a newer side of town, in the parking lot of the Bethel Mall. He thinks he may have stopped the car to go into the Dermatology Clinic. Yes, he thinks he pulled in there to confront Dr. Burke. He doesn't remember facing him though. The doctor must have been too busy to see him. Damn the doctor. Damn Ginnie.

He was eleven years old, orphaned for a year, when he stole money from his grandmother's purse to buy a ticket for the Greyhound bus headed to Montgomery— where he remembered a once-happy life with his parents. But the police found him at the bus station, and called the old man, who dragged him back home and set him in the circle of a spotlight that angled down from the roof of the house. "Sinner, if you want eternal life, make amends!"

He was so mad he wanted to shoot his grandfather. That was the first time he wanted to take a gun to anybody. He calmed down after his sweet-hearted, soft-spoken grandmother forgave him in secret. "You've separated yourself from God, Eddie. But He wants you to return and be united with Him again. That's what your grandfather wants, too. He wants you to return."

Then she made him oatmeal cookies and asked him what else he could expect from a preacher who, for the promise of a grand home in heaven, was out to secure the same for every soul, especially his grandson's?

He hadn't been able to tell her what he expected from his grandfather then; but maybe, and here he sneered at Mal in his mind, maybe the old man in his head—the old man Mal disparaged—could save his soul . . . because despite his complicity in the disparagement of his grandfather, Edmund never truly doubted that he had a soul, and that it needed salvation.

Over the years, Edmund had gone back and forth between conflicting opinions about God and salvation, until he met the psychology professor. Mal, and his buffet of drugs had an immediate effect. Edmund soon took Mal's advice to stay away from his grandparents. Then two years ago, at nearly a hundred years old, both his grandparents died a natural death, one right after the other. The very next day the voice of his grandfather began to taunt him; not in a shout, but a whisper, as if the old man's voice was far away, as if it rose from the bottom of a deep, sealed well. But the whisper didn't last. Little by little, the sound of his grandfather's voice clearly ascended like the rungs of a ladder; coming closer and closer, louder and louder.

Inside his car at the Bethel Mall, his watch says it's four o'clock, but he doesn't know how long he's been here, parked away from the entrance in the shade of a large live oak. He wonders why he's here when Ginnie is at home. Did she send him away? Has he lost her forever?

Oh, you've lost her, Edmund. And now, you risk losing eternal life. Make amends!

He slams the dashboard with a furious fist, and with each hard hit, the old man's words repeat over and over. Make amends.

That must be why he's here—to make amends! He should give Ginnie a gift of compensation, a gift of grand proportion. And he's in just the right place. He gets out of his car to go into the Mall.

Two women hurry out of the Dillard's entrance, heading toward him. He walks slowly, hoping they'll find their car before he has to pass them, but they speed up until they're close enough for him to hear them and see their anxious expressions.

"What I wanna know is who's in charge?" one woman says to the other. She is shaking her head as if speaking of something too horrible to be believed.

"Well, today it's a scary world. Who is in charge of anything these days? You can take all the precautions you want, but things still happen," the other comments. "Mama said she heard on Big Bam radio the guy went crazy and started shooting at everybody in the clinic. Four people were killed for no reason at all. You can't predict something like that."

"Yeah, just innocent bystanders doing their jobs, and some nut-case in a face-mask walks in with a gun."

"What's worse, he got away! Who knows if they'll ever find him?" She gives a depressing sigh. "We live in a dangerous world."

Edmund agrees with the woman, about the world being dangerous. When the two are behind him, he re-arranges the set of his suit coat. One side is heavier than the other, as if that pocket holds something heavy, but it doesn't concern him now. He enters the store to find what he came to find, something much grander than Mal suggested.

At the jewelry counter in Dillard's his hands are jittery. He observes them shaking as he goes through his wallet to hand the girl a credit card for the necklace she's shown him, his gift of amends to Ginnie. He's startled by a scream behind him; a crying baby, pushed by his mother in a stroller. They pass quickly but the scream

49

remains, triggering a memory of many people screaming, yelling, running, and the recollection of a blast, more than one blast.

His hands are trembling so much now, that his fingers seem unable to keep hold of the plastic, and it falls on the glass counter.

"Uh oh," the blonde girl says, cautiously picking up the card with rose-painted nails as if raising a bandage to see if a wound has stopped bleeding. "Want me to swipe it for you?"

Young, pretty, and neatly-dressed, she's trying not to look at his quivering hands. She's probably eighteen, and, more than likely, this is her first real job. He notices the glass counter's shine, and her purse positioned neatly on the floor behind her, next to a bottle of Windex on top of a folded paper towel. He is meticulous too, so he appreciates that about her. He gives an affirmative nod, and she swipes the card through.

"You'll have to sign the receipt, Sir," she says, cautiously offering him a pen. For a second, her gray, gun-colored eyes fix on the center of his tie as if she deciphers something foul in the heart behind it.

Willing his hand to be steady, he nearly snatches the pen, then signs the receipt with jarring strokes: Edmund K. Gillan. Then he feels the need to reaffirm his name. "Edmund K. Gillan," he says loudly, too loudly.

The girl draws back a little, and her defensive movement stirs in him a feeling of pride. Edmund K. Gillan is in charge. Edmund K. Gillan will be remembered.

She hands him his copy of the receipt. "Thank you, Mr. Gillan," she says. "I hope your wife will enjoy the pendant." His wife? How does she know he has a wife? Can't she see he wears no wedding ring?

The girl puts the box into a plastic bag marked with the store's logo and offers it to him. The shaking returns. No matter how much he wills against it, he can't close his fingers around the bag. And now, the girl is studying his tie again, while she holds out his purchased gift—an arm's length away from her breast, as if it's something decomposing and stinking and she wants him to go off with it quickly.

Edmund feels dizzy, out of balance. He steadies himself by seizing the counter's edge, his fingers drumming on it frenziedly. He thinks he's done something terribly wrong. He thinks he ought to go off quickly; he ought not be here, A confusing light from the ceiling falls on the flawless glass of the counter, and within it is the girl's reflection, all crystal clean and golden. He sees goodness in it. He sees innocence. He thinks he sees what he was, and what he is meant to be. And it scares him.

"You keep the gift," he says to her, and quickly walks away.

•

The girl stands frozen, an arm straight out like an angled flagpole, her fingers still holding the bag. She watches Edmund K. Gillan walk frantically toward the

51

main corridor of the Mall, as if certain wickedness tails him.

"I'd like to see something grand, with diamonds," he'd said as soon as he approached the counter and saw her. It was the first time since she'd worked here that someone asked for diamonds, so she wasn't sure she could unlock the glass. She tried the key twice before the display case opened, and then showed him several pieces of glittering jewelry.

He didn't touch any of it, just pointed to the diamond pendant. She thought at the time that there was something wrong with him, the shaking and all. An illness had been her first judgment.

At once, she'd felt compassion, knowing how illness rakes a body. She watches her friend Selena suffer daily. But except for the trembling the man looked physically healthy. He was around thirty and over six feet, a clean-cut sort of dark-haired handsome in a suit of silver gray with a yellow and navy blue striped tie and a white shirt. Except for a reddish smear on the slim band of cuff peeking out of the left sleeve of his coat—maybe from his lunch—the man appeared perfectly dressed, nearly immaculate.

She doesn't know much about older men, but standing in front of the counter, under the light from the ceiling, the deep blue of his eyes, the angular bones of his face, remind her of a picture she once created in her mind of her father; handsome, serious, well-dressed. That was when she was much younger. She has no trumped-up picture of her father now. She's given up imagining

52

him, considers it a waste of her time to even wonder who, or where, he is. But here, in the very place she is standing, a flesh and blood man has given her a gift like none she's ever received.

For a second or two she follows Edmund K. Gillan with a grateful heart, until she comes back to the reality of what she holds in her hand, what he'd told her to keep. Of course, she ought not keep the pendant; it is valued at four thousand dollars, though it had been on sale. She ought to leave her counter and run after him to give it back.

She looks through the store and into what she can see of the bafflingly bright tunnels of the Mall, but Edmund K. Gillan is nowhere in sight. She can't give back the pendant if she can't find the man who gave it to her. Except she knows his name. She can find him if she wants to, in the phone book, or online. Even the credit card company might give her some information if she tells them a customer walked off without his purchase. But it's nearly closing time, and she's tired, and there are things at home she has to deal with that aren't nearly as flawless or beautiful as a diamond pendant she can hold in her hand. And suddenly she wants it, as much as she once wanted her father, as much as she wants her friend Selena to be cured.

Should she even worry about Edmund K. Gillan? She'll probably never meet the man again. He's only one of those undefined and soon-to-be invisible people like her father, who brush against the life of another for reasons only God knows. Except, she's a careful girl who questions her every action, plans ahead, and worries about consequences. Just this morning, she stood in front of her mother wearing a sundress with spaghetti straps, holding a white cotton sweater in her hand. "I can't decide. Should I put this sweater over my dress? With only the straps it's pretty bare, and it is cool in the Mall."

"For God's sake, Alma, you're so cautious," her mother said. "Take a little risk for once in your life." Thou Shalt Take Risks is the first of her mother's Ten Commandments.

So Alma puts the bag holding the diamond into her purse; because of her mother, because it is Friday and her shift is almost over, but mostly because she's off for the weekend and there will be time to decide whether or not to look for Edmund K. Gillan.

•

Edmund stops for an espresso at Starbucks, at the end of the building's south exit. Inside the wintry chill of the Mall, he does not remember that outside, waiting for him, is a gruesome August day, too hot for coffee. When he goes out to the parking lot to find his black sedan he is slapped in the face by the heat, and the coffee splashes on his hand, burning him. He pours it out violently, as if it meant to hurt him, then throws down the cup and smashes it on the pavement with his sole.

He searches one row after another for his car, but can't find it. This time, Mal's voice takes over, reprimanding him: Did you cover your tracks? Did you take note of the car's location when you got out of it? No, you did not. Take charge, Edmund!

After this morning's argument, he tried to do as Mal suggested and take charge of Ginnie. Except, she'd turned her cold blue eyes on him, parted her lips, and called him a lunatic. And then—well, he wasn't sure what happened next. He thinks she became quiet, probably giving him the silent treatment as she was prone to do.

It's possible that he parked his car on the north side, but instead of going through the Mall he walks around the outside of the building that sits like a tremendous replica of a brown toad frozen in a dumping of concrete. He searches for a good thirty minutes, up and down the rank of vehicles; still, he can't find it. Then it comes to him that even if he locates his car, he can't go home to Ginnie without his gift of amends. He paid for the grand thing and its promise of amends, so he ought to return to Dillard's. The fresh-faced girl behind the counter will surely give it back to him.

He turns around for Dillard's, re-winding his way through the automobiles, trucks, and vans, still keeping an eye out for his own black sedan. Inside, at the jewelry counter an older woman is bagging up a purchase. He asks her for the blonde girl. "Oh, she's left for the day," the woman says. "Can I help you?"

He's not sure how he answered the woman, but he finds himself back in the parking lot. The August sun is going down, coloring the multitude of windshields a liquid gold and shooting luminous, fragmented mirrors

55

that cause his eyes to squint and his skin to sweat. He reaches into his pocket for a handkerchief, and his fingers touch something cold and hard—the gun Mal set in his hand last night. He didn't remember taking it out of the locked briefcase in his closet where he'd put it after deciding Mal's idea about scaring Ginnie was a bad one. So why did he take it out? Why?

He stands stark still, as if the soles of his shoes have become part of the pavement. He remembers this morning's violent noise, and Ginnie's sudden silence. He remembers hearing the same noise when he entered the Dermatology Clinic. Yes, he was there. He was there! But he couldn't have used the gun and—no! It's impossible to consider.

He rubs his perspiring forehead, driving his thoughts back to the old pictures on the end table beside the sofa. In his mind, the picture glass lights up like diamonds, and the tarnished brass frames turn to gold. He lowers his head, in memory of his parents, the priest and the missal he gave him. If only he could be like he was back then. An innocent child, a loved child, with none of time's fractures.

Last winter in Beulah, he and Ginnie watched an aberrant snowfall during the night. It made no sound when it descended, and went unnoticed until morning when he snapped up the shade. Then there it was, pure and white; as immaculate as a newborn soul before any human weight has pressed upon it. The snow was only an inch deep—this is Alabama after all—yet it changed everything he could see from the window. The blooming camellias he and Ginnie had planted were no longer blood red. Pine branches bent toward the frozen grass like the silver spruce they'd flocked at Christmas. The steel-colored road in front of their house was frosted-over, slick as glass, mirroring a glint of sun, just a fragment of light drawn around the edges of a high cloud. And when he cracked open the window, the air was chaste and clean.

It hadn't lasted long, the snow. He hadn't expected it would. An hour and the pink and red blooms were brown. The grass had withered, the road was tracked to slush by tires. Ginnie said something about it being impossible to maintain innocence and purity in a tainted world, and he had agreed. But now? Oh, to seize a glimpse of it again!

He wants to go home to Ginnie, but he's afraid of what he'll find, and he has no gift of amends. Wherever his car is, he'll leave it, and turn to Mal, once more. Mal's house is nearby, just across the four-lane that borders the Mall.

He takes off in that direction, running, gasping for breath, dangerously dodging the five o'clock traffic with its roaring sounds, its sirens, and blood-colored lights flashing as if there's been an awful accident. When he reaches the house, he is perspiring profusely. When he knocks on the door, his hands again begin to shake. When Mal ushers him inside, the chill of the Mall returns.

He sits in a chair by the black brick fireplace, still filled with the old ashes of winter, and settles in, a frightened mouse shuddering in a dark, but familiar hole.

"I have things to discuss," he whispers to Mal. "The first thing is Ginnie."

"Mhmh" Mal grins. "Did you show her the gun? Did you do something grand?"

III.

Saturday morning, Alma awakes thinking about Edmund K. Gillan and the diamond pendant he gave her. It is still in her purse, and the thought of finding him to return it is still in her mind. Had it been a miracle? She believes miracles are possible, are the answers to hidden prayers. Her father might show up one day, might even love her, one day, even if she's never seen his face. And her friend Selena might be cured of the leukemia that's sometimes in remission, and other times so debilitating that she doesn't even want Alma's visits. But a diamond pendant? She never prayed for that. She's done nothing to deserve Edmund K. Gillan's gift. And now, the seeing-eye within her soul, the nudging that—so long as she can remember—has mysteriously directed her thoughts, is framing the gift as important, something she must act upon, one way or another.

The smell of bacon frying and the sound of conversation rises from the kitchen of the house she shares with her mother and aunt, who are twins, though surely not identical. Her mother, Moline, is blonde, tall, and indiscriminately tolerant of most anything that passes before her.

Moline said she learned her open-mindedness from her favorite rock star, Chancee Wile. She's been a fan of the aging rocker since fifth grade, even dressed like the bleached blonde woman and received the 'First Place Award for Costume' at a Halloween party. She still has the award-winning costume folded neatly in her bureau drawer, alongside the lacey lingerie and nylon hose she wears beneath one of the two boring, pink polyester uniforms dispensed to her when she began her job as a receptionist in a dental office. Moline puts it there so she can see it every morning, and remember—the chorus of Chancee's Have to Be Me playing in her mind—that life is more than making appointments. When she pulls her expensive lingerie from the drawer—*I have to be me, whatever you fools saaay, this is my day!*—she doesn't consider the danger of having the pointy, metal bustier from the old costume rip into the delicate lace. Moline takes the gamble.

Today in the kitchen is no different. Her mother is talking to her twin and their voices carry all the way up stairs to Alma's room. "Chancee's not timid on stage, or off. That woman enjoys life and never shies from risk."

"But Sister, Sister; are they worthy risks?" Alma's Aunt Pauline is much shorter, rather plump, and, by Moline's standards, stiff as a new broom. "You'd do much better to imitate the mother that raised you than try to behave like some Hollywood-crafted caricature who always looks like she's performing a sex act on stage."

"Pauline!"

"Well, it's true. Your standards are getting as far from what they ought to be as hell is from eternal life."

"Put yourself in Chancee's shoes. She can't worry about things like that when she has to worry about—" Moline says over the sound of water rushing in the sink.

"What, her wardrobe? Reviews?"

"Oh come on, you're too harsh on her. Sure you're not jealous?"

Pauline purses her lips. "Well, I agree with you, Sister," she says at last, her voice playful. "Many a rock star does indeed take a risk."

Alma sometimes thinks Pauline should have been a nun, except a nun has to keep promises. Aunt Pauline isn't much good at that, taking into account she's been married three times; dumping the first for the second, and the second for the third, and the third for a life with her then pregnant, and unmarried, sister Moline— because she loves her sister better than any of them, she often tells her niece. "On the day I learned about you, Alma, my fickle past came to an end." Then she pinches the girl's already rosy cheek.

Their house is ten miles from Bethel, the twins' beloved hometown, and sits on fifty acres of old family land. Bordering the paved county road is a fence with a gate, and a red, dirt road leads up to the house. The land was once a profitable peanut farm, run by the twins' stoic, hard-faced grandfather who had his first heart attack over Pauline's conversion to the Catholic Church —a conversion she undertook at the bequest of her third husband—and his last one, the heart attack that killed him, when Moline gave birth to Alma without being married at all.

Now, part of the land is a chicken-laying business that Pauline runs with the help of José Martinez. Several years back, Father O'Hara, pastor of Sacred Heart Church, the only Catholic Church in the town of Bethel, asked Pauline if she knew of any work for the congregation's newest Mexican family. Pauline said no, but that she and her sister had some vacant land, and she'd been thinking about going into the chicken business, except she wasn't sure she could do all the work herself. So the priest sent out José, a widower, and his daughter, Selena, the same age as Alma. And, on the spot, Pauline had a small staff.

The six-by-three-foot rectangular painted sign that advertises the chicken business stands next to the gate. When they were nine years old, Alma and Selena painted the sign for Jose. It is purple on white, and peeling now, but the misspelled words are still readable: Chickin Eggs. Hole Sale. Or Jist You. Selena had drawn three perfect ovals to advertise the eggs. Only weeks afterward she was too sick to draw.

On Saturdays, Pauline rests from the chickens, leaving them entirely up to José. The dentist office where Moline worked isn't open, so the twins, who are lovers of movies, declared Saturday to be their 'Movie Day.' They allow themselves $4.99 each to buy their choice of an on-demand cable movie, which the other agrees to watch, no matter how much she likes it, or doesn't. When the bill comes, they split it in half, as they split everything, even

61

Alma, who used to think of them as interchangeable mothers. The tables are turning a bit though. Sometimes Alma sees herself as the mother, and the two women as her cantankerous children.

Today, down in the kitchen, Pauline is saying, "I believe I'll choose *Planet of the Apes*," a movie she first came across as a re-run on television.

"*Planet of the Apes* again?" Moline groans. She's standing at the stove, turning the bacon. "We've seen it five times already."

"It's where the world is headed, Sister; certain self-destruction. We can never be too prepared for the end of man as we know him."

"I declare Pauline, you talk about my standards, but you surely have a distorted view of the world's future. Anyway, *Planet of the Apes* is science fiction. It didn't happen, and won't!"

"Not yet." Pauline sits at the kitchen table and puts her napkin in her lap as if she's in a restaurant waiting to be served.

"Not ever."

"Well then, what's your pick? No, don't tell me; I know. It's *Silence of the Lambs*."

"What if it is?" Moline sets a plate of eggs and bacon in front of her sister.

Pauline gives a giddy laugh. "Ha! It proves my point —intelligent people taking instruction from an evil man who will obviously end up in hell."

"How do you know where he'll end up? He solved the case, didn't he?"

"Yes, because evil knows evil. The man ate people, Sister!"

Alma is wearing her red flannel Christmas pajamas, the ones imprinted with snowmen, when she comes downstairs and into this conversation. There is a hole in one knee from where she snagged it on a wire in the chicken house, helping José throw out some feed early one morning. She pressed a patch on it, but it has come off and now the hole has widened. Last month, Pauline promised to sew it up; of course, that never happened.

"Good morning, sleepyhead." Pauline smiles at Alma as she enters the kitchen, and her mother sets another plate of eggs and bacon on the table.

"Here's your breakfast, sugar. Pauline gathered those eggs yesterday. They're the big ones, so eat up; you're too thin."

Alma sits at the table and turns to Pauline. "Did José say when Selena would be home from the hospital?"

"She may come home today. Oh, what that poor girl has gone through the last few years. How I'd love to take her in my arms, give her a hug, and tell her everything is going to be alright."

Pauline has finished her breakfast and is fiddling with the new remote Moline bought, trying to figure out how to turn on the television. "At least, the treatments are over," Pauline says about Selena, "but the doctor wants to be sure there are no undetected leukemia cells left."

"Maybe she'll be in remission for a while," Alma says, picking up a piece of bacon. "She's been so depressed, and hasn't wanted me to come over in such a long time. I miss her."

Moline arranges her chair at the table so she can see the television. "Trials come to all of us, sugar. Life is risky." She turns to Pauline. Her round, doll-like eyes glisten impishly. "By the way, Sister; is life a risk worth taking?"

"Oh, be quiet. Would you just turn on the TV for me? I can't work this remote you bought."

Instead, Moline reaches for the newspaper. "If you don't mind, I'd like to glance at the news. After all, I was the one who walked all the way to the gate to get it out of the mail box."

Without being asked, Alma takes the rolled-up *Bethel Eagle*, from the kitchen counter and hands it to her mother. When Moline unrolls it, the verse from Genesis about the biblical city of Bethel is set beneath the newspaper's name: How awesome is this place! This is none other than the house of God; this is the gate of heaven.

Whenever she reads that verse, Alma recalls Selena, waking in her hospital room and seeing Alma by her bed. "I had a wonderful dream," Selena had said with a weak smile, "of a stairway that reached from this room up to heaven. And I saw the angels of God going up and down the stairway. One of them took my hand." Then she'd closed her eyes again. At the time, Selena was not in remission, she was only in pain.

Moline is glaring at the front page of the *Bethel Eagle*, her eyes widening. "Lord God Almighty, look at this. A doctor, a nurse, and two patients were murdered. Shot to death right here in Bethel!"

Pauline grabs for the paper. "Not here in Bethel."

"Yes, in Bethel, Sister," Moline says, snatching it back. "I'll read you what it says: A lone gunman in a ski mask entered the Burke Dermatology Clinic yesterday afternoon and shot four innocent people."

"Who was he, the man in the ski mask? Let me see the paper!"

Moline is shaken and staring at the wall, so Pauline takes the newspaper from her. Alma sits next to Pauline and they read the front page story in silence. Then Alma looks up, bewildered.

"Why? Our town is a . . . nice town. Why would a neighbor—?"

"We don't know if he was a neighbor or not," Moline says with uncharacteristic caution, as if she must explain the sense in something senseless. "He might have been some crazy itinerant, off the interstate. That happens you know, more and more every day. Sick people wandering from place to place, without a sane thought in their heads." Then she gives Alma's hand a quick, protective pat. "Aw, don't you worry, sugar. There may be a few crazy sickos, but most people could never kill."

"I beg to differ, Sister," Pauline says in a corrective tone. "Does the Bible call Cain a crazy sicko? No. It says he killed his own brother because he was resentful of him. He wanted what his brother had. Jealousy is a human flaw. We're all capable of it—just as we all have the capability to kill."

"Capability, yes. But not all of us do it. I say he was born to be evil. And if he's killed once, he could kill again."

Pauline says she has to agree with the statement that he could kill again. "But no one is born to be evil, Sister. People are born to be good. It's sin that gets in the way."

Moline returns to her usual rashness. "I don't think sin really exists. Intolerant people made it up."

Pauline's face reddens. "Oh, for heaven's sake, Moline. Do you always have to be so obstinate? Haven't you heard of the Fall of Man? If we're human, we're sinners."

"Well, you're not a sinner." She defends her sister with a look of admiration, but Alma thinks she hears a bit of envy in her mother's voice. "My God, Pauline, nobody goes to Mass, or prays, or helps out at church as much as you do!"

"Sinners go to Mass. Sinners pray, and sometimes sinners do a lot of good. But that doesn't mean we don't have a flawed side to our nature." Then Pauline's face reddens as she shakes the paper in Moline's face. "Sin exists!" Her voice rasps, as if she's spent her last breath. "Read this again and see that it does." She looks to Alma as if for support. "Surely you know that sin exists."

Alma shrugs her shoulders. How would she know? She can't imagine how someone could murder another human being though, and take them from their families, the people who need them. She thinks of her father, who might be dead for all she knows, and of Selena and that the day may come when Alma won't see her again. Then she thinks of Edmund K. Gillan, wondering if he might be as sick as Selena.

"Whether it exists or not, I'm ready to change the subject," Moline says. "Give me the remote, Pauline."

The credit roll to *Silence of the Lambs* flashes on the television across the room and it's quiet for a while, except for the voices as the movie plays:

Dr. Hannibal Lecter: First principles, Clarice. Simplicity. Read Marcus Aurelius. Of each particular thing, ask; what is it in itself? What is its nature? What does he do, this man you seek?

Clarice Starling: He kills women.

Dr. Hannibal Lecter: No, that is incidental. What is the first and principal thing he does, what needs does he serve by killing?

Clarice Starling: Anger, social acceptance, and, uh, sexual frustration—

Dr. Hannibal Lecter: No, he covets. That's his nature. And how do we begin to covet, Clarice? Do we seek out things to covet? Make an effort to answer, now.

Clarice Starling: No. We just—

Dr. Hannibal Lecter: No. We begin by coveting what we see every day. Don't you feel eyes moving over your body, Clarice? And don't your eyes seek out the things you want?

Pauline throws up her hands with a dissonant laugh. "Now that's what I'm talking about, Sister. That's what sin is."

Moline seems frustrated, as if she hasn't actually heard those words from the movie before, or else hadn't paid attention. She hands the remote to her sister. "Oh, alright. Press that little button at the top and turn off the lambs. We'll try *Planet of the Apes* and see if your fantasy about where the world is headed is any better."

Pauline brings up the movie, but not at its beginning. Cornelius is reading from the sacred scrolls of the apes:

"Beware the beast Man, for he is the Devil's pawn. Alone among God's primates, he kills for sport or lust or greed. Yea, he will murder his brother to possess his brother's land. Let him not breed in great numbers, for he will make a desert of his home and yours. Shun him; drive him back into his jungle lair, for he is the harbinger of death."

"The Devil's pawn?" Moline takes in a breath of exhaustion, letting it out as she makes her way to the television to manually turn it off. "After what we read in the paper, I've had enough of this Movie Day!"

Alma rises from the breakfast table. Her mother and aunt are still stunned by the shooting; incomprehensible violence right here in Bethel, the house of God, the gate of heaven. And the movies have made them feel worse. "I'm going to get dressed, and then see if Selena's home," she says.

Neither twin answers, each silently sips her cup of coffee. She touches their shoulders as she passes to go upstairs. In her room, Alma dresses in shorts and a tank top, then looks for her purse. She takes out the diamond pendant. It is beautiful. The shine reminds her of the odd snowfall in Bethel, one night last winter. For a while, every living thing was covered in glittering clean, as if nothing impure or diseased had ever existed. She and Selena had made a small snowman with a smiling face of raisins placed just so. Then, after the snow started to melt, Selena had the idea of saving what was left of the snowman in a Mason jar. The jar of water, still amazingly clean, is on the dresser in Alma's room, beside a statue of the Sacred Heart of Jesus that Pauline gave her.

She thinks again of Edmund K. Gillan, standing in Dillard's, shaking like he had an illness. Maybe he does have an illness, even worse than Selena's leukemia. It's often hard to recognize disease in a person just by looking at them, she thinks. Edmund K. Gillan dressed himself well. He was a nice-looking man, surely sweet to her, and probably kind to his own family. Oh, she can't keep the pendant. It wouldn't be right. She'll have to find him and give it back.

The first thing she tries is the phone book. She opens it to names that begin with 'G,' and there he is: Edmund K. Gillan. His address is 104 Raven Lane, and there's a phone number. She dials it, but no one answers and for some reason, she doesn't think she ought to leave a message. She thinks, instead, that she ought to go there.

She returns the pendant to her purse, and proceeds downstairs. "I'm going to check on Selena and then go into town," she tells her mother and aunt. "Do either of you need anything?"

Their eyes turn in unison toward her. "No, sugar," they say at the same time, still looking disturbed by what's happened in Bethel. Oh, they'll soon come out of it. They'll be arguing, again, by the time she gets back.

She drives the mile to Selena's, but she and her father have not returned from the hospital; or else Selena won't let her father answer the door. His truck is parked beside the house, but sometimes on Saturdays, Pauline lets José use her car. Alma parks in front of the house, so she hadn't noticed if her aunt's car was gone from the garage.

She drives into Bethel, thinking of Selena and the disease that has controlled her for years. Pauline says that our loving God does not inflict pain, yet Selena suffers it. When she was first diagnosed, Selena was angry, so angry she tore up her room, ripping down curtains, breaking lamps, and cursing God in words Alma never thought would pass her lips. Alma was with her every day then, listening to her, stroking her shoulders, and making her favorite drink, milk with Ovaltine. Then one afternoon, things changed. The signs of stress left Selena's face. She put her arms around Alma's neck and said, "I don't blame God anymore. He is with me, here at the gate of heaven."

No driveway leads up to 104 Raven, so Alma parks in front of the house. A ray of sunlight glints off the roof and on its dark peak she notices a bird. She can't tell what kind. But, on second glance, in the sunlight, it

70

looks like a dove. She takes a concrete walkway to the house. On either side of it, there is barely any grass at all, as if the lawn had never been watered.

On the porch of the house, she rings the doorbell, then knocks on the door, worrying what she'll say to Edmund K. Gillan. She's just turning to leave, thinking he's not home, when the door opens. A whiff of something rotten coming from inside the house causes her to step back a little. The man in the threshold is Edmund K. Gillan all right, but not the neatly-dressed man she met at the Mall. He's wearing pajamas, his hair is uncombed, and he's sweating profusely as if there's no air-conditioning inside the house. His skin, sallow as peanut butter, seems to hang on the bones of his face, and he stares at her with blank eyes, glazed over. Of course, it is Saturday morning; he must have slept late.

"I'm so sorry to have disturbed you, Mr. Gillan," she says, trying not to inhale the revolting odor. "Do you remember me? You gave me the pendant you bought for your wife. I'd like to return it. I mean I can't keep it—"

"The gift of amends?" His voice is excited, but hoarse, as if he's been shouting or crying.

She decides that he must be awfully sick, maybe even terminally sick like Selena. He hadn't known what he was doing when he gave her the diamond. Now, she only wants to give it back to him and leave. But he looks so ill. Is he being taken care of? Should she call 911? Would that be the right thing to do?

He's trembling, just the way he did in the Mall, and the smell coming from the house is growing stronger, the worst of stenches, a sort of festering decay. It can't be a good place for a man as sick as Edmund K. Gillan.

"You have the gift?"

"Yes, I have the gift. I want to return it." She reaches into her purse and takes out the box.

Impolitely, he snatches it from her and goes back inside the house to what looks like, from the porch, a small, dark library off the living room.

"Ginnie!" he calls to someone lying on a sofa. A woman, Alma thinks, but the room is shadowed. "Ginnie, I'm sorry, so sorry." He's crying now, his head bent over the woman lying stiffly on the sofa. She doesn't say a word, though Alma thinks her eyes are open. Maybe she's sick, too; both of them sick like Selena with some awful disease.

"Can I help, Mr. Gillan?" she asks.

There is no answer except his sobbing, and even from the porch, she can no longer stand the escaping, putrid smell. Gently, she pulls the door closed and goes to her car. Once inside, she takes her cell phone from her purse and calls 911.

"There's something wrong at 104 Raven Lane," she tells the operator. "A man and his wife are very sick. I think someone should come quickly."

She waits in the car, peering through the windshield at the sky. She notices two elongated contrails of airplanes, and if she strains hard enough they seem to converge into the shape of a pale yellow cross.

The standard responders, an ambulance from Beulah Hospital, a fire truck, a police car; all spin around the corner, sirens raging. A police officer and the paramedics rush up to the house. One of them knocks on the door. Edmund K. Gillan stumbles onto the porch as if he's barely alive. She mutters a prayer for him; he's so sadly ill.

The police officer goes into the house, but comes out quickly. He takes a pad from his pocket and strides to Alma's car. "Are you the person who called?"

"Yes, I thought I'd better. Mr. Edmund K. Gillan and his wife are very sick." She glances toward the porch. The paramedics are ushering Mr. Gillan into the ambulance, just as the dove on the roof flies down to the grass-less yard. "Is Mrs. Gillan all right? She's inside the house, too. "

He responds curtly. "Yes, she's inside." He writes down Alma's name, address, and phone number, and thanks her for looking out for a neighbor. "You can go now," he says.

She turns on the car's ignition and watches him go back into the foul-smelling house.

On the way home, she thinks of yesterday's shooting, wondering if her mother and aunt have gotten over the shock that it happened in their beloved Bethel, at

73

Heaven's Gate. Then she thinks of Selena and the leukemia destroying her, and of Edmund K. Gillan and his wife—poor people. Tomorrow she'll call Beulah Hospital to see how they are getting along. Maybe she'll even go visit them, and then, afterward, she'll drive to their house and see if she can save what's left of the grass.

The Psalm of David Fowler

One afternoon before *it* happened—he was in the back yard, poking the rake into a pile of burning leaves. Laura called to him from the porch, "Don't let that fire get out of hand and burn the house down!"

A stream of smoke spread across the yard—not in his direction; it advanced toward her. She covered her eyes. "You shouldn't be burning leaves in the first place, David. They protect the grass from a freeze."

"What freeze? We may never have one." It was the middle of December and South Georgia weather was characteristically kind with a temperature in the low seventies.

"We always have at least one freeze. And remember last year? It was so cold the pipes burst, and we were without water for a week!"

He gave her a condescending shake of his head. "I've got it under control, baby." Then he remounted the riding mower.

"Don't go off and leave that fire burning!"

Even over the sound of the mower, he could hear her warning. He advanced up the yard anyway. All around him dry leaves fluttered and fell rain-like over the yard, while flames from the unattended pile began to lick up, higher and higher.

"Don't you ever think about the consequences?" she shouted as he turned the corner of the house. He knew she'd run for the hose.

The day *it* happened, she asked him the same question about consequences, then she ran into the bedroom, locked the door, and cried. One year later, he, David Fowler, entered the gates of a federal prison, a consequence far beyond his imagining.

He was immediately strip-searched, a procedure that scooped from him the last adhering particle of dignity he'd been able to hold on to since his sentencing, and generated in his mind words he'd heard decades before, as an altar boy serving Mass: I am a worm, not a man; the scorn of men, despised by the people. All who see me scoff at me; they mock me with parted lips, they wag their heads.

As a twelve year-old boy, dressed in his floor-length black cassock and white surplice, the words meant nothing to him then. Not until today when he was ordered by a female guard to remove his clothes, his T-shirt, his underwear; when he was ordered to bend over for her coarse, gloved intrusion of his body; did he genuinely absorb them.

He despaired of ever feeling human again. In place of his dignity, rose a ghost-like aura of obscurity that pressed upon the back of his neck and slumped his shoulders. It came naturally, well before he learned it was the prison posture expected of him.

David Fowler had been the owner of a construction company, and a good man, too—at least until recently, he thought. But the Grand Jury saw him quite differently and issued a criminal indictment, spelling the end of his days as free man. Three years they'd given him for Fraud.

"Aberrant behavior" his defense lawyer argued, not typical of his client's career, or his record of civic and charitable contributions. "David Fowler acted out of desperation. The only consequence he considered was that his floundering business would be salvaged. "

It wasn't exactly aberrant behavior. He's always spoken of it as a trait he was born with, a trait Laura consistently warned him about: the tendency to light a fire and then go off, leaving it burning unattended. She warned him, too, about the consequences of trying to grow Rise Construction too fast and to excessive proportions, but he hadn't listened. He bought new equipment, more trucks, a larger, more elaborate office building, and increased the number of his employees. Every two weeks he found himself scraping to make payroll, and finally despaired when he saw making payroll was no longer possible. That was when *it* all began, on a Friday night at The Checkmate Lounge.

He'd wrapped himself into the vinyl shadows of the farthest booth in the corner, so he could still watch the door. The black and white tiled floor spread before him like a large checker board, until his eyes became accustomed to the dim, blurred shadows. An emergent pyramid of light crept across the game board from the opening door, and the shadows transformed into people. But the men who entered were not the ones he was waiting for.

He pressed his fingers into the vinyl seat—it gave a little, like toned skin—took another swallow of Scotch, jabbed another cigarette into the ashtray, stirring the ashes around with the butt then pushing them to the side until he could see the glass bottom. He should leave. They had kept him waiting too long, an hour already, and he didn't want to give the impression he was desperate. If he waited any longer, they would assume more than he wanted them to; but if he left, he might miss his chance to save Rise. Even worse, they might not come at all.

He lit another cigarette. Intermittent spasms of laughter buffeted his indecisive thoughts. A young waitress bent close to him, questioning him with her eyes. Yes, he'd have another Scotch, he said, imagining the look of her body underneath the black shorts and red T-shirt with its checkerboard logo. She reminded him of the girl pictured on a magazine page, which one of his workers had torn out and then tacked up in the portable john at one of the construction sights, except the picture had left no work for the imagination.

The waitress pulled a pad of paper from the pocket of her shorts, wrote down his order, and retreated across the tile floor, her long legs in their tinted hose moving like game pieces over the black and white squares. Watching her walk away, his purpose for coming to the Checkmate only intensified. His own life seemed to be walking away from him. Soon, he would be out of business, just when he needed to prove to himself and to Laura, that he was still in control. The once familiar looks of respect from men, the fawning and admiration from women, had become less frequent. Even the waitress, who was very young, probably noticed the marks of his age—his wash of gray hair, the bulge of his gut— and thought him insignificant.

Over the last few years, he'd hooked some big jobs, quite a few of them, through his association with the man he was waiting for, Victor Dooley. Through these jobs he'd overcome setbacks, too; but now, the business was suffering greater losses than any he'd ever had. It looked as if it might sink. He had to crank it up again. His workers, as well as Laura and his children, depended on him to provide.

And wasn't that what a man was supposed to do-- provide for his family? "But if anyone does not provide for his relatives, and especially for members of his household, he has denied the faith and is worse than an unbeliever." Those were words he'd also heard at Mass, and so they must be true. Except sometimes truth has to be bowed—just a little—to shoot the arrow beyond the aim of what a 'good' man might ordinarily do.

Laura wouldn't agree though. She'd throw the whole business overboard and watch it get swallowed up rather than make any sensible concessions to Dooley, a man she thought to be unscrupulous. She didn't know that over the last fifteen years, he'd already made a number of sensible concessions to the long-serving Chairman of the County Commission. Well, if she wants to eat at restaurants three nights a week, if she wants regular vacations and all the fixings, if they are going to keep the children in private schools, if they are going to keep them from a lifetime of college debt—if all of this, then he'd have to make allowances again, or else Rise Construction would go to hell.

Victor Dooley's phone call, earlier in the week, dropped redemption within arm's length. "I'm meeting with some people at the Checkmate on Friday, happy hour time. You know. It's about the Elkhardt deal, something with a little twist you might be interested in."

"What's the twist?"

"We'll talk when I see you."

But in another call that came a few hours later, Dooley had hinted, in his usual way, that Rise would get some new construction jobs out of old man Elkhardt, a big investor who'd sold the county two blocks of run-down buildings in the downtown area. Dooley's plan was to make them into new county offices and social service agencies, but some complications had cropped up after his re-election. The commission wore some new faces, and some of the faces wanted to advertise the bid outside the county. Since Dooley won by the skin of his teeth, he was under scrutiny. His opponents investigated Dooley's every step, but David knew that being under scrutiny was not something a politician enjoyed. Dooley had said as much, said he was resorting to "new ways" of getting things done, ways made necessary by his opponents' oppressive eyes. David wasn't sure he could count on Dooley anymore. Still, as he watched Rise's numbers sink, whatever the man had in mind seemed to be exactly what the business needed, so he'd ended up at the Checkmate.

The door opened again, and two men and a woman entered. A few heads—his included—turned without shame, to take note of the woman, who could give the model in the magazine picture hanging in the john some real competition. Of course, this woman had clothes on. She wore a purple dress that Laura would have called "tawdry"—one of her favorite words whenever she caught him glancing at another female. But this woman with long, wavy red hair and a figure that rated a ten, was worthy of more than a glance. He breathed deeply to put himself at ease. A lot depended on his ability to seem indifferent.

Victor Dooley, a big man with a football player's neck and a politician's manner, reached him first, and stuck out a hand. He introduced the younger man with him as Jeff Finn. David recognized Finn from the newspaper; he was one of the newly-elected faces on the county commission. Finn ran against his opponent promising 'New Ways for Old Things.'

"And this pretty woman here is Sandra Bobber," Dooley said. The woman reached over to shake David's hand, and held it longer than he would have expected.

The young waitress in the red T-shirt reappeared. David noticed that she gave him a look of anticipation, so he took charge and ordered a round of drinks. Dooley cocked his head and peered sideways at the waitress through half-lowered lids, then mumbled something to her that David didn't catch. The girl's face went slack. She quickly wrote down the order, then turned on her heels and walked off with her chin in the air.

Finn and Sandra sat across from David. Dooley shoved in next to him and jumped on the subject immediately. "We gonna get you the bid on Elkhardt,"

Dooley said, glancing across the table at Finn. The thin young man seemed ill-at-ease, but nodded affirmatively, as if he was experienced enough to be where he was. Dooley gave a throaty laugh. "But here's the twist--one you'll enjoy, I'm sure. Sandra goes with it."

Sandra hadn't taken her eyes off David since they were introduced. Her gaze made him even more uncomfortable than her lengthy handshake.

"What do you mean?" David asked.

"Finn's idea." Dooley took in a few short breaths of guttural air that counted for laughter. "I thought we'd have trouble with the new political crowd, but hell, they're hungrier than we are!"

Finn flushed, then opened his mouth as if he was going to speak, but Dooley overlapped whatever it was. "Finn knows you and me been calling ourselves 'friends.' He ain't adverse to that. Fact is, he don't think it's enough."

Finn fidgeted with the ashtray as he addressed David. "Mr. Fowler, if you would be, uh, be interested in something such as we are, uh, proposing, we would be prepared to make it, uh, more lucrative as far as the compensation that, uh, I believe you've had in your past affiliation with Mr. Dooley."

"More lucrative!" Dooley hee-hawed. "Don't he have a way with words?"

Finn sniffed, looking innocent as an altar boy. "Now, Miss Bobber figures into this. As you might imagine, that is why, uh, she is present."

"How does she figure in?"

"Well, as you know, there are certain specs on any job that are open to variance in costs."

"Damn," Dooley interrupted. "Get to the point!"

At once, Sandra leaned across the table. "I am the point, Mr. Fowler. You will hire me and I will see to it that you, as well as the three of us, receive more than enough compensation from the Elkhardt construction project."

"You're talking about changing figures?" David took in a short, quick breath, tried not to let them see his sudden dizziness.

"Yes." Finn answered with a breath of relief. Just as David gloated to himself that 'New Ways for Old Things' had been a good slogan for him.

"Don't play the naïve one, Fowler," Dooley said, then eyed David cautiously, but neither spoke for a few moments.

Dooley's patronizing look didn't touch David, who saw the whole thing for what it was. Calling back favors was one thing, but what they were talking about was nothing less than the misappropriation of county funds. Of course, he wouldn't involve himself in anything like that. Still, to satisfy his curiosity, he asked, "How would it work?"

Sandra reached across the table to put a hand on his arm. "I simply come to you for a job that will entail much more than just the Elkhardt Complex. I will assist with any other contracts you may be handling. You can be assured my resume is impressive. I have lots of experience."

"Look Fowler," Dooley took a gulp of his drink and wiped his mouth on his sleeve. "We just gonna make some adjustments. To some of the numbers. Nothing out of the ordinary."

"Look, uh, I mean, they practically teach you this in the MBA program. Some, um, executives from national companies do this all the time," Finn piped in, the smart boy in class.

"Yeah, and some executives go to jail for doing it, too!" David said, a little too loudly.

At once, Dooley looked around the room to see if anyone had heard. "Well then, maybe we ought to talk to somebody else about Elkhardt." He took a long swallow of his drink. "Maybe you don't need no more business. Or maybe you're playing cute—the immaculate little choir boy—to impress Sandra." Dooley gave Sandra a commanding look.

"Oh, he'll come to the right decision," Sandra said. She squeezed David's arm again and ran her tongue over her bottom lip. She had full lips, painted bright red for the occasion. Laura would say she had signs of a prostitute, and David would agree; Sandra was a bit hard to swallow.

"Bridgeman, Finn's my witness to this conversation." Dooley tipped his forehead toward the younger commissioner. "Finn knows what he's heard. Future reference, ya know, in case it's needed. With that said, you go on and think. Lemme know Monday morning."

"I'll let you know."

Nothing else in their conversation pertained to Elkhardt until Dooley got up to leave. "Some advice," he said. "You'd be smart to go along. Hey," and here he leaned in close, "Sandra's sharp as a tack. Ain't nobody gonna know."

David thought he saw a flicker of solicitude in Dooley's eyes, but it disappeared quickly when he slapped Finn on the back and said it was time to go. Sandra laid a hand on the middle of the table. Pouting a little, she said, "I do have a lot of experience." And then, she followed them out.

David sank back into the booth. With everyone else gone he found himself easing up a bit. Maybe it wasn't the best way to do it, but if it would save his business—.

He'd called Dooley on Monday. He'd gone along. He'd gone along with Sandra Bobber, too. The lawyer even brought her up in Fowler's defense, said that David had asked Sandra again and again about numbers, after they had engaged in their consensual acts, but she kept from him anything specific. More than that, the lawyer portrayed Fowler as the lonesome husband alienated from his wife, trying hard to preserve his business for her sake in spite of it all. David had to swear to Laura, again and again, that he hadn't consented to the lawyer's sob story.

Worse, Finn lied on the stand, as Dooley had warned he would do if David tried to implicate any of them in the plan to misuse county money. Victor, Sandra, and Finn went free, while the jury gave David Fowler a three year sentence, and the papers had a feast over what every leading article called a "slap on the wrist."

At least he'd had Christmas at home, however strained. He and Laura barely spoke as they decorated the tree. Silence had become their habit during the time surrounding his trial and sentencing, voiceless shadows slinking into corners to avoid each other. She, from anger. He, from shame.

He thought the two oldest girls, Marnie and Morgan, noticed the lack of communication between their parents when the four of them set out their sparse Santa Claus for little David Jr.

"It's too quiet in here," Morgan said. "I feel like we're in church." David smiled, remembering how often Morgan had to be carried out of Mass when she was younger, for talking. He noticed that Laura smiled, too, until her eyes moistened and she left the room.

To keep the children from reading about "it" in the newspaper, or hearing about "it" from a friend, Laura told the children their father would be out of town for a while doing consulting work, and that she was taking them to their grandparents' home in Florida for a visit. His oldest daughter, Marnie, hadn't bought the consultation story. He could tell by the teen-age sneer she gave him. He assumed it was only because she liked visiting her grandparents that she let it go without comment. But he knew that it was only a matter of time before an internet search told her what he wouldn't.

He watched Laura pack the children's clothes, and then her own silky, sunset-colored things, things that he might never see again. Would she leave him for good? She went somewhere else, somewhere far inside that he could not access, when she learned he'd cooked the books. Never had he seen such disbelief in her face.

"Why didn't you refuse to do it, David? You knew it was wrong."

He could have refused, and lost the business. He could have blown the whistle on Dooley, too, which could have landed him work or connections with the man's opponents. He'd taken a risk, because . . . why? Because he had always understood the importance of taking risks, had always looked down on those who toed the line and considered themselves upstanding moral citizens. He'd never been afraid of his own shadow, like some of those he worked with. Risk had lifted him to the top in his profession. But now, it had pitched him to the bottom. Strange that such a character trait could work both ways.

Two days after his family's departure, he left to serve his sentence. His lawyer told him he was lucky, three years in a minimum security prison that served as temporary home to a long list of American Who's Who. His words, his lawyer's words—"almost a country-club atmosphere"—were laughable after he spent his first night in the place.

It was true that the place housed an elitist group of white-collar 'felons' (how that word made his throat close) and that during the small amount of free time that he had (free time?) he'd met two former state senators, a couple of judges, the former governor of another southern state, and tens of executives. He didn't know why any of them were in prison. No one ever discussed reasons; he'd learned that by asking around on his first day.

During his free time he began to walk with one of the ex-senators. After a few months, they were walking eight circular fenced miles in a matter of minutes. But while his muscles grew hard, David's emotions grew soft, so soft that he found himself crying over anything. The open sky's sunset. A gentle rain. Even a red-winged blackbird lying dead in the grass.

Beyond the prison fence stretched a pasture with a few gray donkeys, a couple of hogs, and a handful of peacocks. Frequently, one of the peacocks would shake itself violently, spread its tail, and begin to strut before the prisoners, proudly flexing his iridescent blue-green plumes. David first stepped back, gasping a little at the beauty, but then he froze when the plume's black circles, like judging eyes, waved his way.

"I'd like to be proud as that bird again," the senator said one day, his words, almost a whisper.

"Yeah, I was thinking the same thing," David said, though he still couldn't look at the thing for fear of its black-circle eyes.

"How much longer have you got in here?"

"Two hundred and eighty six days."

"I've only got thirty," the senator said. His eyes turned to look at the gate, as if he feared it. "I don't know what I'll do when I get out. I can't practice law anymore, and my wife divorced me. But hell, I don't blame her." He paused to look at David. "What about your wife?"

He was angry with Laura and her lack of communication with him since his sentencing. Even if she should get in touch with him, he wanted her to know how badly her obvious absence has made him feel, and that he's not likely to forgive it. But he answered the senator, "I don't know. I'd like to think she'll forgive me."

The senator guffawed. "Then you'd better re-invent yourself, son. As a rule, women don't care for felons."

The prison also housed another smaller group of exceptionally angry men who insisted they were innocent of all charges and claims, who damned the judges who sentenced them. Then there were the young prisoners, many in their teens or early twenties. During recreational hours and meals David took stock of them; unwanted street kids. One of them even told David, as they shot free throws together, that he almost preferred prison to the life he'd previously known. David looked twice, to be sure the kid wasn't joking. But his expression remained the same strange admixture of defeat and comfort.

David played basketball with some of them when he first arrived, but once, during a boisterous game, he broke a finger. He didn't let on though; he'd heard too many tales about the prison doctors. The finger has healed now, though it's bent and barely usable.

While groups with similar backgrounds banded together in free time, the accommodations frustrated all efforts at elitism. In a room that held cubicles to pair fifty men, David's bunk was above a batty, old man named Raphael, a wiped-out farmer who had lied on an application for a mortgage loan on land that had been in his family for a hundred years. He'd gotten twenty-five years for Mortgage Fraud, one of the few inmates who talked about the reason he was here. He'd already served twenty of those years.

Raphael was, by his own boisterous assessment, "A man with a plan. That's what I am." He sat up in his bunk most of the night playing out his strategy for the new cotton farm he would buy when he got out.

"Cotton's rising. You read the papers?"

"Try not to," David said, thinking of his children, who had surely read the newspapers' editions of his story, and of Laura, who'd made no attempt to visit him, or write to him. He'd called her on several occasions, when inmates were permitted 'phone visits.' She never answered. For a while, he wrote to her daily, but after he received no letters in return, he maintained the awful silence. If she wasn't going to make a move, then neither would he. But perhaps she had. Perhaps she had moved on.

"Good times is coming," Raphael went on. "Invest your money, now!" he repeated, night after night.

Finally, David leaned over the side of his bunk. "Shut up, old man. You're dreaming."

"Ain't no dream. I already found the land, made fine for cotton by the Lord our God."

"Is the Lord going to give you the money?"

"Do you think he won't? The Lord forgives. And He's got plenty of money. Fact is, it's all His, no matter whose pocket it's in."

The old man was one of the oldest prisoners, and came across as too backward for most of the inmates that David knew. Rafe had few friends as far as he could tell; yet he was rarely seen without a smile that crinkled up only one side of his face, causing the eye on that side to constantly squint, and the one on the other to drag downward, giving him the look of derangement.

David shook his head as if amused. He actually liked the old man's trust in simplicity, and in an uncomplicated world where right was right, wrong was wrong, and people could be forgiven. It was the same idea he had—when he was young and innocent. Now, he knew it was as irrational as Rafe appeared to be.

"Go to sleep, Rafe," he said.

"I'm gonna sleep like a baby dreaming of my farm. What you gonna dream about, son?"

David could think of no answer. The World of David Fowler wasn't a world of happy dreams. It was plainly defective, ruled by greed and competition; a dangerous world where every person ahead of him was his enemy, and where a so-called friend, a Judas, might slice a knife down his back for money.

And forgiveness? Well, just consider Laura's lack of it.

Because his prison record documented his management skills, he was assigned work in the financial office—nothing but filing and some other clerical work at first. Still the job was a plum compared to lawn or laundry maintenance.

The financial office was located outside of the main gate, and a few other inmates worked there, transported daily by a small van. The filing system had been in a shamble, so David cleared it up, and made a friend of his supervisor, Mr. Flagg, a family man about David's age. Flagg was a welcome relief from the prison guards who seemed to take no small pleasure in tormenting those inmates who were once well-to-do. Flagg offered him the use of an old, blue bike, and gave him permission to ride it to other office buildings, delivering and picking up mail.

On one particular delivery, David came into the office and stopped dead in the doorway. He thought the woman standing at Flagg's desk was Laura. Her copper hair was tied back with a ribbon, and the slope of her shoulder was made for the palm of his hand. When the woman turned a profile, David saw that he'd made a mistake, but even then, his spontaneous reaction was to make a move on her. That had always been his first reaction to any beautiful woman; imagining what it would be like to have sex with her. A reaction he hadn't worked hard to stem. Just sex though, he'd say to himself. Laura was the only woman he would ever make love to. With a few exceptions, like Sandra Bobber, he had been loyal, but his wife had no idea about any of his discreet betrayals, maybe because he kept them so discreet that he himself forgot most of them within a few weeks. If she had uncovered his infidelities, she'd have left him long ago.

The eyes of the copper-haired woman dwelled for a time on his face, then fell to his prison garb, and cut quickly away. He felt her look like a hard blow that lowered him to the earth. Then she moved toward the door, and he noticed her eyes were on him again. He strained to decipher her movements: was she attracted or terrified? He was sure he saw some mutual attraction until she pulled the door closed behind her. He decided then that she was only curious. He was an oddity to her —a revolting oddity. Not a man, but a worm.

Back in his bunk after the lights were out, he thought again of the slope of the woman's shoulder, and then

Laura's shoulder, bare and cool to his touch. What was it in him that burned so intensely at the thought of a woman's body, any woman's body? How powerful was the itch—having nothing to do with love—that caused him to toss away any scruple to satisfy himself for a brief moment. Was it the same itch that caused him to illegally change figures for the promise of a whole lot of money for his company? Whatever sort of itch it was, it had destroyed his life. Still, he wondered: if his life wasn't in ruins, and if he felt that itch again, would he be reckless enough to ignore the consequences for another scratch?

After the incident with the office woman who had left him low, he started to look at himself. Had his ambition to provide for his family really been reckless? She didn't know why he wore the prison clothes. She didn't know why he'd done what he did. Through her eyes, he saw a different David. A worm and no man.

The guards watered his self-description daily. One of them, a short man with eyes like a hungry dog seeking bones as well as shoulders broad as a Pit Bull's, seemed to take a distinct dislike to David on the first day he entered prison, and the mongrel kept it up until now. David was on the blue Schwinn, delivering mail, when the stocky guard intentionally sprang in front of him, causing him to swerve and fall to the pavement. The guard stood above him and laughed. "You ain't the big man you thought you were, are you, Fowler?"

He wanted to say something from the psalm about 'the power of a dog,' but he gave no response. Mouthing-off at a guard could land him in isolation. After that, his head and neck began to extend even further forward, like a wandering turtle's, and the hunch of his shoulders compressed, expecting the lash of insult. When the senator was set free, the old, white-haired, former prince of the nation walked through the gate to freedom with the same stoop and elongated neck. David thought he would always be able to recognize a man who'd been in prison by the slump of his shoulders and the jut of his head.

After the senator left, he spent more time with Rafe, a man who was rarely down. Surprisingly David's mood became lighter, too.

For all the years the old farmer had been here, his only job had been cleaning the tables, chairs, and bathrooms in the visiting area used by wives and children—some wives and children; not David's, and not Rafe's—who came to visit the inmates. The senator once told him that Rafe had begged for the job. Sitting across from each other, at a table in the long, dining room, David asked him why.

"You don't see it. They don't see it either, the visitors. But I minister to them people, them poor children and wives--out there on their own when somebody promised to take care of 'em. I clean up their messes while they're here. It's the least I can do. Can't do it for my own no more."

He wanted to ask about Rafe's family then; what happened to them; but the old man was giving him his cock-eyed smile, a smile that always made David want to grin, too. He didn't want to spoil that little bit of joy.

Rafe rolled up a piece of thin ham from his plate and stuck it in his mouth, chewing as he spoke. "Betcha half of them families left all alone don't have food this good to eat."

Left all alone? He hadn't thought about that in the context of his own family. He hadn't thought about their day to day existence. Just before he entered the prison, he turned over all his accounts to Laura, knowing there was barely anything in them. He figured her parents would help. But how selfish was that? Not any of them —Laura, the children, or her parents, had done anything wrong, yet they were paying for his mistakes as much as he was—maybe more. Like a child dared to jump over a campfire, he'd closed his own eyes, to what he was actually doing when he mishandled the books, and then soothing the burns he'd received with an excuse he was only trying to provide for them. Now, he saw that was not only an excuse; it was a lie, a goddamned lie. His image, his ego was what he was really worried about. Laura knew him well enough to know that, too. No wonder she wouldn't forgive him.

He glanced across the table, wondering about Rafe's wife. The old man liked to talk about the families who came to the visiting room, but he never talked about his own family. Did he even have a wife, or children?

David decided to ask him. "Who visits you, Rafe? I mean from your family." He knew at once, he'd asked the wrong thing when Rafe's smile disappeared, "Just the one I saved. Comes every year or so. He's grateful."

"A son?"

"He's the only chile I got now. Rest of 'em burned up when their momma set fire to the house," He stuck a spoon into his glass and stirred his tea as if his statement had been about the weather. Then he spooned out a

95

lemon slice from the tea glass, popped it into his mouth and rolled it around, sucking on it a few seconds—no grimace at all—and spit it onto his plate.

David stared. Inconceivable! Did Rafe mean his wife had burned up her own kids? But the old farmer seemed to misinterpret David's stunned expression.

"Just cleaning my palate," he said explaining the lemon. "Try it sometimes. It's the real bitter stuff that cleans ya up the best."

"Wait, you said your wife burned down your house-- intentionally?"

"I reckon she wanted to collect some insurance so she could pay some bills and get away. Happened after I was here, 'bout nineteen years ago." Rafe didn't seem sad or angry, only matter-of-fact; but again, David was floored.

"And the rest of your children died in the fire?"

Rafe nodded. This time he lowered his chin to his chest. "They say my baby girl—she was ten year old— lived a couple a days in the hospital, but she was burned so bad she must not of wanted to live any more. They let me out for the funerals. Five funerals, in one day."

David shook his head in sad disbelief. "Your wife and four children."

"Nope. Five children. My wife got away. Police went looking for her; but hell, she was gone like the flame on a blown-out candle."

"But you said you saved one, the one who comes to visit you. If you were here then, how did you . . . "

"Didn't save him from the fire. He was the only one still out in the fields that day. I saved him from prison, else he'd a been here instead of me."

"Do you mean that he was the one who falsified the loan—not you?"

Rafe nodded. "Changed the figures after I'd signed it. I reckon he thought he was helping—John Bruner's his name, my oldest boy. I didn't say nothing though. He was my blood. People do for their blood. You know that."

That night in his bunk above Rafe, he studied the ceiling and its sad shadows, many shifting shadows created by men passing a few floor lights that kept the dorm room from being totally dark. It was mind-blowing that Rafe had allowed himself to be here when he could have kept it from happening. What had made him so forgiving? So loving?

David's thoughts traveled back to his own beginnings, to his youth as an altar boy, to his college days when he met Laura and fell in love. He went over every detail of their wedding that he could remember—six bridesmaids, six groomsman, and Laura in her white dress with seeded pearls all over it, looking like a princess. He recalled the night Marnie was born, and later, Morgan, and then, David, Jr. He loved each of them, but was it enough to suffer through prison—suffer innocently—as Rafe was doing? And what about Laura? David was angry because she was ignoring him when he needed her —*he needed*. He hadn't considered that she might be needing him.

And then, for some reason—maybe a repositioning shadow---his thoughts retreated to Father Keating, the priest who'd trained him as an altar boy. "Every time you serve at Mass you are helping Jesus perform a miracle.

He could do it without you, but he wants you to be a part of it," the sandy-haired Irishman had told him.

He was ten years old when he became an altar boy, and he was proud to be one—at first because he liked seeing his name in the church bulletin for the next Sunday's 6am Mass. His mother never had to drag him out of bed for the 6am though; he was always ready and planning ahead, getting early Mass out of the way so he could 'graduate' up to the 10am Mass—because when he got there, he was qualified to do weddings and funerals. And that was where the money was. The year he turned fourteen, David had made more in six months of serving Mass than he'd made in two years carrying out groceries at Winn Dixie. Weddings, at thirty or forty dollars for an altar boy, were the most productive--unless he told each bride, "You're the most beautiful bride I've ever seen!" That was an easy fifty bucks. Father Keating had actually suggested the brown-nosing. He couldn't imagine what Father Keating would suggest now, if he saw him in this place.

He must have made some soulful noise then, maybe a sigh, because Rafe called up to him. "Talk to the Lord, son. Be a friend to Jesus and He'll make you new."

"New as an altar boy?"

"I reckon," Rafe said, "though I ain't never been a altar boy. I'm a hard-shelled Baptist. But here, it don't matter what you are. Church is church, and church can save ya soul. Lotsa people find the grace a' God in here."

Before prison, David scoffed at reports of inmates finding God in jail, especially the young Texas woman he once saw on television. Now, he recalled there'd been no slump of her shoulders as she marched to the death chamber, praying for her persecutors and the souls of the two people she'd cruelly killed. She said it was by God's grace she could do that, but David had written it off as nothing more than a last ditch attempt for the Governor's sympathy and a stay of execution.

"We're goin' to church on Sunday; you and me," Rafe said. "So you can go on to sleep."

On Sunday, Rafe dragged him to the prison chapel. "I see it's Catholic today." Rafe said, sounding disappointed as they entered the triangular room, painted white, where Mass was going on. "You don't know til you get here what it'll be."

The priest was giving a homily, and many of the young Hispanic men were weeping. The first words David actually heard came during the Responsorial Psalm, words he'd never grasped as an altar boy. "My God, My God, why have you forsaken me?"

Rafe's shoulder trembled beside him. The old man was sobbing softly. David touched his shoulder and found his thoughts turning to Laura. He'd call her again, keep calling and calling until she answered, and he could tell how sorry he was for what he'd done—to her.

That night in the dormitory room, instead of the shadows, he studied the light on the ceiling—a pale bluish, widening beam. Actually beautiful, he thought. The first beauty he'd found within the prison walls. He'd called Laura again, just after Mass, and was amazed when she answered. The sound of her voice, fragile as thinly spun glass, pierced his heart. Over and over, he'd said he was sorry. And over and over, she condemned what he'd done. But she had answered his call, and that was a step.

He must have made some audible sound, because at once, Raphael's ruddy face popped up from the lower bunk.

"Quit that crying, son! It ain't over 'til the fat lady sings. You'll get out one day. Then the Lord and me are gonna let you in on our cotton farm. So raise your hand and believe it!"

He lifted his hand with the broken finger until he could see it distinctly in the beam of light, and then raised it high. Any future he'd have might be as misshapen as that finger; but in this present moment, a light shined in the darkness of his prison, and David Fowler smiled.

The Mercy Seat

Today is Good Friday. It is my turn with Grandmother. Her gray hair is spread out upon the pillow like roots from an old tree. She lies sleeping in her hospital bed, in a room of clinically accurate monitors, IV poles, and bed rails. To someone looking in, she might seem insignificant, barely separable from the sheets drawn tightly around her like swaddling. Yet she is the most consequential person in my unworthy life. She is church to me, salve for a sinner.

From her window on the second floor, across Bell Street, is a view of the crumbled parking lot where the church used to be; Saint Mary Magdalene, Grandmother's church, the church of my Catholic family. It was built of white brick on the corner of Main Street back when Main was lined with huge oaks hovering like protective parents over everything below. In our small town Catholic children were armed with the sacraments and the Catechism, raised to defend the Pope, Confession, and Natural Family Planning. "Defend your church with courage," Grandmother instructed us, "because the Lord wants you to be a saint." Our footfalls behind hers, on the sidewalk after morning Mass, became as one melodic phrase, tapping out yeses for our conductor. Because of her, I kept in line. I didn't lie, or cheat, or deceive. But that was then. I am not a child anymore.

Her eyes flick open as if she's remembered something important. "Did you make the six o'clock Mass at St. Mag?" Her sense of the present continues to disassemble.

My eyes return to the crumbling lot. "It's Good Friday. There is no Mass on Good Friday."

She taps a finger on the side of the bed, in rhythm with the heart monitor. Tick, tock, tock, tick. Its out-of-sync sound bounces off the hospital walls. She gives me a look of condescension, a familiar expression from those days at St. Mag's. "I know it's Good Friday, Theresa."

I recall another Good Friday, hurrying with her from the parking lot to the church entrance. Her hand is on the small of my back as she pushes me gently toward the double-paneled doors. I don't like that she does this, don't like her insistence that I'm timid and won't go inside without her. Lifting the old latch soiled by a legion of other hands, I shove open the door and our shadows pour themselves down the wine-colored carpet. We are barely in time for the Way of the Cross, where we'll stand, where we'll genuflect and kneel, considering the great cost of our salvation. I go through the motions with her, wishing to be somewhere else. After the last station, when Jesus is laid in the tomb, I happily collapse into the pew.

Grandmother nudges me. "Get up. Be respectful."

Benediction comes next. Father Tim swings the censer.

Tick, tock.

Tick, tock. The heart monitor continues.

Grandmother is awake and worried about the Easter Dinner, a meal she's always tended to as unfailingly as she tended the old church. "The dressing should be done early, and put into the refrigerator."

"It's done. Mother has seen to it."

"We will not eat until three?"

I assure her that we will not.

"Father Tim must have time to rest after the noon Mass."

Father Tim is Grandmother's son. Her dearly beloved son. Her favorite child. My mother tells me she's always known this. Still, it is she who spends hours with Grandmother, reading to her, talking to her, praying with her. Surprisingly, Father Tim seems unable to cope with death.

My mother started coping with it when my father died ten years ago. Father Tim presided at the funeral Mass. "How comforting it must be to have a priest in the family," people said, as though to put the duties of consolation on him. My mother gave a flat smile to some, and confided to others that his presence was no comfort. I thought her attitude toward her brother odd. Surely he would have reminded my mother about eternal life. Surely he would have pointed to the promise of salvation. Had he been remiss in not doing so? Yet, he's faithful to the vows of his vocation, while others are not.

Every morning, after he says early Mass at the new church, a church that is miles and years from Grandmother, Father Tim comes to give his mother Holy Communion and visit a while. His is the first shift in our twenty-four hour relay of staying with Grandmother, so when I arrived this morning, he was there.

I waited outside the open door while Grandmother was questioning him about death as if he, above all, should know the answer. Years ago, when he was ordained, when he took his place above them, she and my mother erased his humanity. Now, he is cautious in his answers, maybe because he knows there's no room for error. He told her that we will all die, some sooner than others. Then he spoke of the soul's mysterious journey to God.

Grandmother gave him a look of derision. "Before long, I'll know all about the mystery of death *myself*. The pity is, I won't be able to give you the answer."

He lowered his head like a child cornered into confession. "I'm sorry, Mama."

She reached for him then, because she loves him in spite of his inability to give her the answers she wants. He took her hand, and held it to his lips until she dozed off, then he came out into the hallway.

"Hello, Theresa." He touched my shoulder because I'm his niece, but also because I'm one of the flock he's vowed to tend. "I didn't see you and John at the Holy Thursday service. Maybe tonight at the Veneration?"

"John's been working late, and there's the baby. There's no nursery for the Veneration."

Excuses, I'm sure he was thinking. But they were more than excuses; they were lies. John, though he is hard-working, didn't work last night. He kept the baby so I could go to Holy Thursday Mass. Except that's not where I went. And tonight, he'll keep the baby again, but I won't be at the Veneration.

"Well, God knows your reasons," Father Tim said. There was an uncomfortable pause, as if he expected me to tell him what my real reasons were, and then a quick kiss on my cheek. He took a few steps, then turned back. "I meant to tell you, Theresa. I'm hearing Easter confessions at four this afternoon. Several people requested it."

"I've already been to Confession."

Lying is easy when you've done so much of it. But still, in his presence, the lies never lacked a heightened sting. Father Tim looked as if he wanted to challenge me, and it's possible he knows the truth. But how could he? I've been incredibly careful.

"Good,' Father Tim said. "Everyone needs confession. I'll see you back here on Sunday for the Easter Dinner soon as Mass is over." He walked down the hall, and disappeared around a corner.

Now, Grandmother wakes and looks in my direction. "Oh, it's you, Theresa," she says, evidently disappointed at seeing me instead of her son. "Where's Father Tim?"

"He's probably back at the rectory by now."

"He shouldn't come so often; a priest has so much to do." She takes in a labored breath. "I think I hurt his feelings when he was here. I hope he's forgiven me."

"Oh, Grandmother. You don't need forgiveness."

The derisive look she gave to Father Tim crosses her face again. "There's no one alive who doesn't need forgiveness."

How can I respond to that? Except, she still holds the baton, expecting harmonious acquiescence, expecting more courage than I can give her. "Yes," is all I can come up with.

A nurse enters. "Hello, honey," she says to grandmother and presses three fingers on her wrist to the beat of her pulse.

"Mrs. Donelly." Grandmother corrects her, with a sense of propriety as strong as ever. But her voice is weaker than yesterday, weaker every day she's been here, battling a malady no one has named.

"Mrs. Donelly then," the nurse retorts, as if she doesn't like being told what to do. She doesn't look at Grandmother. She straightens the baby blue sheets, picks off a speck of dust from the black name tag attached to her starched, white uniform. Then she moves to the foot of Grandmother's bed to update her chart, glancing up at the heart monitor with pen in hand. Her cold efficiency reminds me of someone I know too well . . . someone I wish I didn't know.

"Is she getting better?" I ask.

"She's ninety-seven. We can't cure her of *that*," the nurse says flippantly, as though grandmother is so hard of hearing that she won't hear *that*. "We're just trying to make her comfortable."

Grandmother gives her a scornful smile. "Comfortable enough for death?" Whatever else she means to say is lost in the abrupt spasm of a cough. I put an arm around her shoulder until she stops.

The nurse reaches into the pocket of her uniform for a small bottle and syringe. "Can you hold her arm, honey," she says, but she doesn't wait for me to do it. She gives the injection without looking at either of us, her lips as straight as a ruler's edge.

"What if she were *your* grandmother?" I ask.

She sniffs, snaps the chart shut as if some things happen only to other people, then leaves the room as if she's done all she needs to do.

I start after her, to go down the hall to the Nursing Station and complain about the merciless woman who betrays the heart of her vocation. Except I turn back. Who am I to judge a betrayal of heart? Who am I to judge the mercy of others? If Grandmother knew what I've done, she'd tell me exactly who I am. But then, she'd expect a resurrection—and I can't accomplish that.

Grandmother shows me her hand with the IV. It's begun to bleed, so I press the call button beside her on the bed, hoping it doesn't bring the nurse who just left. It doesn't. This one's a male, and he spends at least half an hour patiently re-inserting a new IV in her other hand. By the time he's finished, she's exhausted, and nearly moon-colored. Still, she musters a thank you. He smiles and leaves the room.

"He was a merciful young man," she says. Then, motioning me closer, she whispers, "It's possible that he's a saint."

I was nine, 'half-grown' according to Grandmother, when she first spoke of sainthood. Like a card player unfolding a deck, she laid holy cards with pictures of saints on the azalea-colored bedspread. One mystical face after another. Some reflected peace, others were distorted with doubt, and maybe even the fear of death. Always, I looked away from them.

"God wants you to be a saint, too." Her voice was strong then, like the bells at Mass. But a saint was the last thing on earth I wanted to be.

"I'm not that good."

She stroked my hair. "Oh, you're more than you think you are. Remember Mary Magdalene?"

I'd nodded, yes. As a child, my understanding of Mary Magdalene was simply that she was the saint our church was named for. Years later, I learned that Mary Magdalene was a sinner before she was a saint, but I had no interest in her conversion or how she came to it. As for the church that bore her name--it was built just before World War II. After the war, there were few men left to watch over it, so the church was tended by extraordinary women like Grandmother and ministered by staunch Irish priests. It grew from a fragile embryo in a Southern Baptist town intolerant of anything Catholic into a cornerstone of the community. Except for me, it was always only a building. It was simply there, and always would be.

Today, only the broken pavement of its parking lot is left, an expanse of puzzle-like pieces appropriate for someone, like me, who's fallen far from the mystical faces on holy cards, far from the saint Grandmother wanted me to become.

Her eyes are on mine. "I love you, Theresa."

"I love you, too, Grandmother." One of the few truths in my life. That *she* can love *me*, is the surprising thing. She knows I'm imperfect, but she doesn't know the depth of my—of what she would call my *sins*.

"Remember the mercy seat," she says, as if she's heard my thoughts.

As a child, I often spent the night in Grandmother's house, in a rose-colored room, wrapped in the sweet-smelling sheets of a high bed with four posts to square off its corners. I woke to the smell of bacon popping in sync with the sound of a song. Every day, the same hymn of repentance.

Lord, at Thy mercy seat, humbly I fall;
Pleading Thy promise sweet, Lord, hear my call;
Now let Thy work begin, oh, make me pure within,
Cleanse me from Every sin, Jesus, my all.

The old Protestant hymn was one her husband, my grandfather, used to sing daily. He converted to the

Catholic faith a year before he died. And on his death bed, he was humming that hymn.

For over a year, I wasn't close to repentance; not close to giving up a man I thought was everything my ordinary husband wasn't: better looking, better at sex, better at making money. Today, though, it's no longer those attractions that bind me to him. It's the power he has over me—the power I've given him—and dread of how he might use it.

Early afternoon. Grandmother is sleeping again. Like clockwork, my mother slowly tiptoes in to take my place beside the bed. Hers is the longest shift in our relay. She's brought her purple canvas bag, a symbol of her vigils, packed with the usual sustenance: books, a bag of chips, and a blue sweater she's knitting for my infant son. Four months ago, he was born here in this hospital. Grandmother was here, too, because she'd broken a hip. She was the first person to snuggle my son, yet now, there are times she doesn't remember him at all.

My mother, Alice, is a small woman with dark but graying hair. I look like her; she looks like Grandmother. She takes her place in the brown vinyl chair that turns into a bed, a chair from which she performs acts of mercy for Grandmother. For the last three nights she's slept in the chair beside her mother. The chair is too big for her. It would fit Father Tim, but he hasn't used it. My mother would never ask him to. When I volunteered to stay nights in her place she said I belonged at home with John. "You can't have a good marriage if you spend too many nights away from each other." My mother's statement shames me. A good marriage is what John *believes* he has.

She unpacks her bag, and sets the chips and books on a shelf in the small closet. In a low voice, so as not to wake Grandmother, she says, "Go on home, Theresa. I'm sure John needs you, after working all day for such an unpleasant boss." A statement, out of the blue, one that causes me to take in a breath.

"How do you know John's boss?"

She takes out her knitting and sits in the chair. "Oh, I know more than you think. You should hear what they say about him at my Bridge Club. Andrew Toole may be a nice-looking man, and he's certainly very wealthy, but his CPA firm is, at best, unethical. And now he thinks he's good enough to run for mayor, which would—and I'm sure you've spoken with him about this--leave John to do all the work. Oh, I wish you'd encourage your husband to find another job!" Then she eyes me cautiously, as she often does when she's noticed negligence.

"John is good at his job, Mother. And he likes it." I don't tell her that for a long time now I've hoped John would change jobs, too. Yet I think she senses it.

"Go on home to your husband," she says.

I kiss her goodbye, and then kiss Grandmother's forehead gently so as not to wake her, and step toward the door.

"Pay attention to the turkey," my mother warns. The turkey is my contribution to the Easter dinner. "Baste it, or it will be too dry to eat."

I walk to the disintegrating lot where my car is parked. My footsteps tap out the song about mercy. It plays and replays in my thoughts. Neither the hymn, nor the old St. Mag church, will let me go.

St. Mary Magdalene Church was torn down when I was a freshman in college. Easter Break of my senior year, I returned to a new church, constructed in a new place. The old one had been as ordinary as my husband, John; the new one, as formidable as my glitzy lover. Even then I was impressed by grandiosity, and didn't miss the old church.

But now, in the splintered parking lot, I wonder about its death. Was it demolished piece by piece, as it was built? Or crumbled to dust with one massive blow of betrayal? And what of the ancient Oaks, encircling like soldiers—were they cut down without a thought for the faithful wind blowing through their branches, and then shoveled away in the teeth of heavy machinery that ripped up and dismantled their roots? So intricate were those living roots! How magical they were as hiding places for colorful eggs at Easter!

It was Grandmother who boiled, dyed, and hid those eggs. Plastic was never an option for her, only real eggs. Then came the year she watched me pass over the plain-colored ones, looking for the prize, the one wrapped in gold foil. In the end, my basket was empty and I was in tears.

Grandmother held me close. "I hope you learned a lesson." I had no inkling of what she meant then.

Now, standing in the center of the broken parking lot where the marble altar used to be, the meaning is clear. All my life I've neglected the plain and true for a spur-of-the-moment extravagance. Again and again I've played this game, and again and again I'm left with only shame and remorse. For John—how I've deceived him—and for my infant son—a gift, despite how he came to be. His father is not John. His father is Andrew, John's powerful boss, a man I met in the new church, a man I thought a gold-foiled prize, better in every way than my steadfast husband. No one knows this. It would dismantle my family. It would demolish John.

It's six-thirty on Friday night. I'm irritated because John is an hour and a half late coming home from work. The baby is in his crib fussing for a bottle, and when John walks into the kitchen, I'm hurrying to mix up some macaroni and cheese. "Where were you?" I ask, slamming a lid on the pot of boiling macaroni.

"Where do you think I was? I was working."

"Well, Veneration is at seven."

"Veneration?"

"You said you'd keep the baby."

"Oh yes, so you could go." He looks at the wall clock. "Are you?"

"I suppose it's too late now. Will you give the baby his bottle?" I don't wait for his answer. I take an already-made bottle of formula from the refrigerator, run it under hot water, and hand it to him. "Why were you so late?"

"Andrew and I were talking about my assuming some of his clients, to free him up a little for the election."

Every mention of Andrew elicits a little shiver that starts in my heart and runs down to the ball of my left heel—guilt, with my one, usual consolation: Andrew isn't married, so at least I'm not *the other woman.* Except now, and maybe for the first time, I realize the silliness of that excuse. Mine is the greater risk; the only marriage in danger of being demolished is my own. This is not what I want, not what I set out to do four years ago when John and I made vows at St. Mag's.

"But Andrew's already given you more than you can handle, hasn't he?"

"I do have a lot on my plate, but it's not more than I can handle. At least, not yet." John is looking me square in the face; apprehensively, as if he's unsure of what else he wants to say. Then the baby cries loudly, and he leaves with the bottle.

On the night I had to tell him I was pregnant, I was worried. He'd expect excitement from me. Could I play that part? I must have played it well enough though, because if he thought otherwise, he didn't show it. He only kept saying, "I love you, Theresa. I love you." And he loved my son, too, from the moment he was born, never doubting the baby was his.

But when I told Andrew, he drew back like a snake in an S-curve, his neck and head lifted as if ready to strike. "How far along are you?"

"Three months."

"Three months," he repeated, and began to calculate. Then he recalled that he sent John out of town on a lengthy business trip around the time the conception *probably* took place. There was nothing even remotely kin to kindness in his manner, only his usual manipulation. "Taking a paternity test is out of the question for me. With the campaign coming up, every move I make will be watched and then reported. So figure a way to get one from John—use his toothbrush or something. After you get the results, call me and I'll decide what to do."

I thought he'd do one of two things—insist on an abortion, or take my son from me. The thought of either made me literally ill. But I agreed to, somehow, get John's DNA and have it tested. I never did---I didn't need to; I knew what the test would show.

I waited a week or two and then telephoned Andrew's office on a private line. As soon as he picked up, he directed me to "Hold on a minute," as if I was a tiresome intrusion. In the background, I heard a man's voice: "When are you gonna announce? You know you gotta start early." I felt certain he was asking about Andrew's planned campaign. It was a good time to butt in because I knew Andrew would be listening more to them, than to me, so I blurted it out. "The baby isn't yours. It's John's." But he was giving someone else an order. "Set up the announcement for Thursday. And I need a crowd of people there. Hand out favors if you have to, but get'em there!" I wasn't sure he'd heard what I'd said until he came back to me in a harsh whisper, "Is that what the test showed?"

"Yes."

"Good. That's the kind of crap I *don't* need. Not now." His tone was venomous.

Though I was afraid he would, Andrew never asked to *see* the results of the non-existent test. A week later, when he had the time and enough of an itch for sex to discount the chance of discovery, we went on as usual in our spotty affair. But I was taking a chance, too, and for what? Momentary gratification, as usual? When the baby began to move inside me, I couldn't look John straight in the eye. Still can't.

On Holy Saturday, I take the turkey from the refrigerator where it's been thawing for days. I wash it and pat it dry, rub it with butter as the package advises, and then put it in the oven. John is on the long blue sofa with the baby propped beside him.

"I'm going to the hospital early," I say. "Father Tim has to prepare for the Easter Vigil and can't take his turn." For once, it's not a lie.

"I'll keep an eye on the turkey," he says, shaking a red rattle just beyond the baby's reach.

Before the door closes I turn to catch a glimpse of them; their movements stalled, the morning light playing on their faces like an Impressionist painting. Only the *impression* of a father playing with his son. I wish I could make it real.

That night, I make a pot roast, mashed potatoes, gravy, and fresh peas—John's favorite meal. I turn down the overhead chandelier, light candles, and, when he comes into the dining room, I kiss him. He pulls back a little, lifts his chin as if my kiss has made him uneasy. "John," I say, reaching for his hand, to assure him of my love. I do love him—for being so much more than I am.

The phone rings then, a call from Father Tim reminding John to let the hospital know we'll need an extra table for tomorrow's Easter dinner. Or so my husband says after he hangs up the receiver.

He stands before me, his hands on my shoulders. Even in his touch, I feel anxiousness. "Theresa, tomorrow is Easter, a new day for you, for me, and for *our baby*." Have I imagined he emphasized 'our baby'? "And I think we should start referring to him by name. We don't, you know. You call him the baby, or my son, and I call him little man. But he has a fine name and we ought to use it."

"Of course," I say. "Joshua then."

He lets go of my shoulders and resumes his place at the table. "Joshua," he repeats, giving the name validity.

Easter Sunday. We gather in Grandmother's room. Father Tim has brought his favorite potted flower, a white lily. He hands it to me. "The sign of a repentant soul," he says. A drop of perspiration slides down my temple then slips to a petal when I take the plant from him. I set it on the extra table John has procured.

My mother has set the table with crystal, china, sterling silverware, and white napkins with tatted lace. There's a folding chair for each of us, except

117

Grandmother, who will use the hospital tray extended over her bed. My little son lies on a pillow next to her, squirming like an overturned turtle. She touches his fingers and smiles. He plays with her hair, bark-colored strands clinched in his miniature fist. "Little lamb of God," Grandmother whispers and kisses his forehead.

"The Alpha and the Omega," Father Tim says. "Now that's a picture, isn't it?"

John stands in the middle of the room like a load-bearing beam, his eyes on the baby he used to call 'little man.' He looks handsome in his Easter suit and tie, but ill at ease again. Something uncertain is coming.

As if she's been cued, my mother rises from the brown, vinyl chair and goes to the hospital bed. She leans over Grandmother, and peers into Joshua's small face as if she sees something significant there. "Do you think Joshua resembles you, John?" she asks. "I'm just not sure."

I hold my breath. My mother is sly, her discerning eyes like flashlights probing a dark room.

Father Tim shifts from one foot to the other to ground himself, just as I've seen him do before he enters the Confessional. He lays a hand on my shoulder in priestly empathy. "Often a son doesn't resemble his father. I see much of Theresa in him."

John stiffens, as if his load has become heavier. "I'm happy for him to resemble only Theresa and no one else."

"What does it matter? He's an image of The Father," Grandmother says, kissing him again. "And mine were the first arms to hold you, Joshua." At once, she's remembered what I thought she'd forgotten. Too quickly though, she re-enters the past. She turns to me. "I've finished sewing your Easter dress for the egg hunt, Theresa." Her voice is quivering now, barely audible; even a few sentences seem to tire her. "It's mint green, with a three-layered skirt, and little pink rosebuds embroidered on each tier."

My first instinct is to steer her back to the present, but in this room, the present is becoming unpredictable. I have a sense of something secretive going on, something verging on exposure. So I go back with her, reproaching myself; it took her weeks to sew the dress, and still, I'd thought it ordinary.

She motions me nearer, shadowing Joshua's face with a thin arm. "I've hidden a plain-colored egg in the roots of the tallest oak." She points toward the window, a childlike twinkle in her eyes. "Brush away the old leaves."

My mother's eyes fill. It's hard for her to watch her mother diminish. She leans into Father Tim. He puts an arm around her, and his eyes fill, too.

"Go on, Theresa," Grandmother insists.

I step toward the window.

"Do you see it? The plain one?"

I see nothing except the broken parking lot below, but I answer, "Yes."

"Good. Choose that one. It's worth more than you think."

119

She smiles at her great-grandson, and he returns it readily, as if they shared a riddle of great consequence. And then she looks up at me, her face as mystical as the saints' on her holy cards. Naturally, I turn away. But Grandmother won't let me go.

"Theresa," she whispers, her eyes examining mine. "We know the truth."

"All of us," my mother adds quickly. "Even John."

My heart stops. They're talking about Andrew and me. But how could they know? Andrew is a powerful man in the community, and from the start he was adamant about our being discreet. I raise my eyebrows, as if I don't understand. It's easy to do; by now, pretense is practically a second-nature. "What do you mean?"

The flashlight in my mother's eyes manifests itself, no longer probing, but directed. "I mean the truth about your affair with John's boss. Just admit it, Theresa, and then get rid of it," she says, as if it was as simple as taking a garbage can out to the street.

A tattered breath escapes, coming from somewhere deep, somewhere in the vicinity of my heart. How is John reacting? But his eyes avoid mine. All their eyes avoid mine. As though searching for a shared target, their eyes turn toward Joshua. Surely they couldn't know Andrew is his father! For a few excruciatingly long seconds, I am silent. Then I try denial, my next best defense. "I don't know what you're talking about. I barely know Andrew." But there's far too much familiarity in my pronouncement of his name.

"Theresa, I've heard enough confessions to recognize infidelity," Father Tim says. Had he heard Andrew's confession? Of course, he'd never say if he had. My uncle lays a hand on my shoulder. "Acknowledge it. Let the work begin."

There is nowhere to hide. I collapse into the brown vinyl chair, the mercy seat my mother uses for her vigils, burying my face in my hands so I don't have to see judgment in their eyes. Then the words free themselves, take flight on their own. "I was wrong, so wrong."

Though I don't look up, I know John is standing above me. "I didn't mean to hurt you, I never wanted anyone to know, but…" The simple truth flees from my charge, and can't be summoned back. "Andrew is the baby's father." And I wait for his justifiable condemnation.

"Look up. Look at us, Theresa," Father Tim says firmly. "The only one who doesn't know the baby is Andrew's is Andrew. But we've all decided to keep quiet about it. I mean if that's what you want. You have to make the decision."

It *is* what I want. If he ever finds out, Andrew has the power to take Joshua from me. And he might, because the gold-foiled man is no prize, no prize, at all.

I raise my eyes to John and see pain in his expression, hurt that I've caused! Yet he is here, *still* here. Oddly, I think of Mary Magdalene on the one holy card that always puzzled me as a child. Mary Magdalene peering up at someone or something hidden from view. Now I know the object of her gaze--one who's suffered for her. "Yes, it's what I want. John and Joshua, only them."

John bends to take my hands, steadying my rise from the chair. "And we want you, Theresa," he says, wrapping me in his arms.

My mother tucks back a strand of my hair and kisses my cheek. "Stop crying. "

Father Tim reaches into his coat pocket for a handkerchief, and hands it to me with one of his winks. Somehow this one speaks nothing of his characteristic humor. Somehow even his wink spills mercy. His head motions me to come with him into the bathroom. I follow, and, closing the door behind us he sits on the tub edge, motioning toward the turned-down toilet seat. He unfolds a bright purple stole. I say the words, the simple words. And he says his, his simple words.

When he opens the door everyone is conveniently occupied; but even with their eyes averted, I feel my face flush. I'm sure it's scarlet red.

"Happy Easter, Mama," my mother says, pulling Grandmother's tray over to the bed.

Grandmother waves her away. "Take the baby, Alice. I have to go change the altar linens at St. Mag's, and then prepare the children for First Communion."

My mother takes Joshua from beside her with a sympathetic smile, going along with Grandmother's unpredictable, and ever-escalating flight into the past. "All right, Mama," she says, "as long as you eat your Easter dinner before you leave for the church."

And so we eat, talking to Grandmother in the same high-pitched tones we use with Joshua. She looks at us as if we have no sense and then says, "The turkey is a little dry."

I expect my mother to agree, instead she says, "The turkey is just perfect, Theresa. I'll make turkey soup from the leftovers and bring some tomorrow."

Father Tim says he won't be able to come tomorrow; the Bishop will be visiting. My mother gives me a look that says *I knew it.* John loosens his tie and leans back in his chair. It all seems miraculously normal, but I don't know how it can be...so simple. The feeling frightens me a bit, because there's one, more complicated thing left to do.

We clear the silver and china. We re-fold the lace. We pack up the leftover turkey, to be made into something new. I kiss my mother, Father Tim, and then, Grandmother. She whispers in my ear, "Did you fill your basket today?" I notice she is smiling.

"Yes, it's full, Grandmother."

She gives a slight sigh of relief. "Well, you've been quite a slow learner, Theresa."

John, Joshua, and I proceed to the broken parking lot. Between its cracks, acorns round as tiny eggs have begun to sprout sprigs of green.

At home, we take Joshua to the nursery to get him ready for bed. John plays peek-a-boo with the baby blanket my mother has crocheted for him, while Joshua coos back with a toothless smile. I take the opportunity to leave the room and go to the telephone. Andrew's voice, flashy even on the other end of a receiver, sounds reassured when I call for an ending.

"It's best. To be honest with you I've been meaning to bring this up—but then we, well, you know. Still, it's best. It might have blown up in my face one day. I'm sure you've heard I'm running for office," he says, with no emotion for me, and still no mention of Joshua. I hang up the receiver, feeling sanitized.

I stand at the door to the nursery. Joshua is babbling in his crib, dressed in his footed pajamas imprinted with blue Easter bunnies. I notice John has changed, too, into his simple clothes. He stands beside the crib; his face is serious, his eyes on Joshua, but his mind appears to be somewhere else. Is he thinking that I made a fool of him? Has he come to his senses, wondering how he will live with me now, let alone love me again?

Except when he sees me he opens his arms. And when he makes love to me it is sweet and satisfying. John is the treasure. John was always the treasure. And in his welcoming embrace, in his merciful love, I am so much more than I thought I could be.

Blue Bird of Happiness

Halloween. Old Florida Highway 98. Right turn toward the Gulf, a procedural deviation from integrity. Procedure is programmed into the mind of a physician. Even some deaths are scheduled.

The sun roof is open and the windows down. I turn the Lexus into the parking lot of The Boat Dock Bar, crushing primeval oyster shells beneath Michelin Energy tires while triangular flags slap plastic, carrot-colored polka dots against a hallowed, sapphire sky, and an incongruent blast of music shuts out the pious breath of waves.

There are lots of bars in Destin, but this one is set apart. The Boat Dock Bar claimed her Gulf-front spot when the town was just another Florida fishing hole, and then held to it, regenerating like the tail of a lizard after Hurricane Dennis.

When the hurricane hit, my wife, Felicia, heard about The Boat Dock's fate and called from her law office to tell me. Four people in plastic masks, drunk enough to think they could ride out the hurricane on a walkway with weak railings, were swallowed by the sea.

The walkway was the bar's first renovation. Crossing the wood planks, I pass a memorial sign that reads: 'To

125

the Flawed and Fallen,' and I'm envious of the bar's resurrection. An outside voice enters in. *Envy is normal and shouldn't be suppressed. It simply needs to be properly channeled.* A lesson I learned in Group Therapy. Never mind the maternal negation in my head —that envy is a cardinal sin opening the soul to greater vices.

I didn't have time for a change of clothes, so I'm still dressed in a pair of new khaki shorts I paid eighty-five dollars for at the outlet two weekends ago, the last time I was down here. I wear no socks with my loafers, no underwear for easy disrobing, and no shave since I left Birmingham. A wealthy woman I met here once—a woman with hungry eyes, but too old for me—summed me up by saying I had a neat, charmingly passive, appearance. I doubt she would say the same today; there's a salsa splatter on my expensive Polo shirt from a drive-in lunch on the way down, and then a swerve of the Lexus to avoid the unavoidable. The armadillo threw itself in front of the wheels while I was taking a bite of my Taco.

The walkway to the bar leads to both indoor and outdoor refreshment. Outside, on the deck surrounding three sides of The Boat Dock, some kid swaggers in a baseball cap and flashy sneakers while he hoses off an abundance of sea gull droppings. Those birds, free to fly wherever they want, scavenge the fishermen's nets, snatch bits and pieces of flesh, and leave their excrement scattered across the rails and decks of bars. Like me, such birds create procedure, the need for a daily dose of stinging water.

The music on the deck is loud, but not loud enough to detach one from the cleansing going on. I move inside where the bar is crowded, where the tables are few but the plastic is plentiful: Halloween masks. Fine with me; I don't like to contend with inquiring faces. I'm timid as a dove, a Jonah flying from accountability. If I could find the right outgoing ship, I'd flee to Tarshish myself.

I check my Rolex to keep on point. It's five thirty-two in the afternoon; time enough for necessary introductions and a little conversation beforehand.

I wedge into a ten-inch space beside a half-screened partition that thatches the boats in the harbor into dots of soft color and indistinct outlines. It reminds me of the original Seurat my wife, Felicia, hung in my Birmingham office. She positioned it directly across from the framed Hippocratic Oath. In an afternoon sun, the light bends, the glass reflects the fire-like color of opals, and distorts the words I swore to: Do No Harm.

The sun purples the windows of The Boat Dock, brushes against a cafeteria display of bodies, still-life props parading contradiction; perfume and suntan oil, Gucci summer ensembles and K-Mart cut-offs with halter tops. An unattractive waitress, in short overalls and flip flops, comes close enough for a kiss as she takes my order.

A Tequila with lime.

I scan the more appealing bodies; some standing, some at tables—all in masks. I get into the music, old music with lots of bass, like an opus of mechanical heartbeats.

Waiting for me, a block away, is the over-decorated condo, paid for with proceeds from a few months of moonlighting in the women's clinic where I work—to put it quite frankly—to keep the population under control. I bought the thing for my wife, Felicia, but she's come only once. Her women clients keep her too busy.

At parties with colleagues or over dinner after a difficult day, Felicia likes to say that *both of us* defend women. She goes up against big corporations for her clients and against the men who manipulate and use them. She's proud of herself when she pulls out a favorable, profitable verdict. I go up against tiny babies, scrape a womb, and pull out the pieces. Profitable, yes. But proud of myself? There are days when I can't show my face, days when I'd welcome being swallowed by the hurricane and ingested into the belly of a whale.

The Boat Dock Bar's ceiling is lined with heavy duty fans that stir the Gulf air. Fans line the ceiling of the condo, too, where the air whirls through the blades above a king-sized bed. My procedure is to leave the bed unmade for effortless re-entry, half an hour of therapy. It's an expensive bed, top of the line, allowing for a tourniquet of arms and legs.

The members of my therapy group in Birmingham liked the analogy when I gave it.

"It's like a tourniquet of arms," I'd said. "Keeps the heart from bleeding a red contrition."

"Dr. Bird, I believe you're making progress. The seeking of pleasure gives life its color," our leader said.

In front of me, a gold-masked couple sits at a table for two. She's dressed fashionably, maybe Versace. The undulation of a hand as she talks scatters the sparkle of a sizable diamond ring, and sends the scent of expensive perfume in my direction. Her short, dark hair has a salon sweep of strategically-placed grey. The man with her has on a green plaid Armani shirt with the appropriately classy shorts. She is loud. He is laughing. Their hands touch, their eyes fix on each other. On cue, they drain their glasses, and, in sync, get up to leave. I understand procedures.

They will have sex before the day is over.

I notice a girl across the room. She wears a slim, silver mask, and a thong bathing suit with a little flap to cover a bit of her cheeks. She's young; I'd say about twenty. Already there's cellulite on the backs of her thighs, but it's firmer than the stuff you see on spread-eagle women about to give birth. I've never gotten used to looking at cellulite, it's evidence of corporeal disintegration. The same girl was here two weeks ago. She didn't notice me then. I ended up leaving with somebody a little older, a little tighter. Now, our eyes catch. Today will be different.

Except I think of Felicia sitting across from me at the old Boat Dock those years ago, her fingers stroking my hand, clasping it as if she would never let me go then running it along her body—no cellulite in sight. She talked about our educations, and where I bemoaned the cost, she stated her surety that our "investments" would spell success.

"That's what you want, too; isn't it?" she asked. "You don't need to be shy with me. I won't judge you for wanting the good things in life, dear."

I wanted something greater than that, but I didn't say so. Felicia's always liked accommodating men.

Reflecting on this long-gone day with Felicia, I take the couple's empty table, its glassed-over cedar-top spotted with disturbing pointillisms of light. Maybe I will depart from procedure. Maybe all that the girl with the thong needs is someone to talk to. Maybe that's all I need. She backs into the seat. Says she's sorry, she can't find a place to sit.

I say, "It's okay, sit here." Her bottle of Coors makes a thud on the glass as she flops down.

She takes off her mask and sizes me up. I'm too old for her. She's too young for me. But she lifts her chin and takes a breath as if she's someone I ought to recognize. Her expression says she'd like to know more about me. Do I tell this girl, who resembles so many I've pared from their responsibility in sex that sex is what I'm looking for?

The girl speaks, but the music is too loud for me to hear. Should I invite her out to the deck for a few minutes of fleshing-out conversation, maybe a kiss-and-tell? She could kiss me, and I could tell her my increasing concern that—despite the maternal lesson echoing from my childhood—it's not envy, but spinelessness, that opens the soul to greater vices? No. No, I don't have the backbone for an exposé.

In Group we start with a first name only, to get accustomed to revelation. Some end up spilling their souls, hoping for the confirmation that usually comes; the hugs, the saccharine understanding. I don't really buy into it, but somehow I need it. I'm the only man in the session, and something about my name makes the women happy. So, in group, the women get personal quickly.

I could get personal with this girl. I might say, "Hello, I'm Blue Bird," and wait for her smile at the absurdity of my given name, and then open up a little: "By the time I was born, my mother, Kathryn Bird, was forty-four years old and already had seven children. She'd never have considered the alternative I offer women." The first time I thought about revealing those thoughts in Group, I realized how much I admired my mother.

Felicia and I have no children. She doesn't want any. For almost an entire year Felicia was on the edge, almost revised her stance. But then she took on a big case that demanded twelve hour days.

"A child would mean the end of my career," she said. "Or my career would mean an unhappy child," she added, looking for recognition in my closed eyes.

In the operating room, during procedure, I've often thought about saving one for myself, and even about leaving Felicia and raising it on my own.

Actually, it would be easy to save a child; some procedures miss the mark, leave viable babies on the table. I've felt the clasp of tiny fingers and looked into freshly-opened eyes that seemed to plead—for what? How could they plead for anything, knowing nothing? I turned away while diminutive chests heaved like waves, then quivered to a final unmoving. Contrition? Bleeding red.

Late at night, after a long day dotted with these "incidents," as I was accustomed to record them in the daily medical records, I tried to tell Felicia how I felt. I got up from my desk and led her by the hand to the white leather sofa where she sat beside me. I felt her stiffen as if she knew I was going to say exactly what I said, "I can't do it anymore." Nearly a whisper.

She stood at once, then looked down at me as if I were one of her clients.

"It's only misplaced guilt. Because of how you were raised—by a woman who never made a societal difference." A zing about my mother she never fails to use.

I stood, too, shouting back that she cared only about herself, her comfortable life, and nothing about my happiness. I can't recall now everything I said, except that I did not fail to use the words "small-minded" or "arrogant" several times. My outburst was so uncharacteristic, and unaccommodating, that Felicia flinched.

Felicia doesn't like to see me angry. She doesn't like to put me at too far a distance. When she says she could do just fine without me, she's lying and she knows I know it. She thinks she can appease me with sex; cold and mechanical, eons away from what I truly want. I want to love Felicia the way my father loved my mother. But Felicia has become hard, too hard to love like that.

The girl in The Boat Dock Bar wipes a mustache of sweat from beneath the tiny, gold ornament piercing her nose, and says her Coors bottle is empty. I order another. Someone approaches our table and, unable to conceive of the possibility that she and I might be *together,* asks her to dance. She shakes her head no. She reaches across the table, runs a finger around the brim of my tequila and tastes the salt.

"So, you're a doctor?"

She has on a look of trust that I recognize. So many trusting looks from spread-eagle women who expect some reciprocal words of sanction. I can't give them words. I give them the machinery of my trade; the scalpel, the tools that suck away the undesired, the accident. I can't weigh the procedure with my heart, or measure it with my integrity. If I did, I couldn't continue.

I keep my heart out of Group, too. I don't speak of my once-wayward father, or say that he lifted my mother in penitential arms, and re-dedicated himself to her as a man of conviction. I don't mention the stir in my chest, a stir that returns when I enter into the memory. I don't mention my desire to be like him—and not myself.

Last week in Group we were asked about family. I gave only names. "My mother gave all her children 'bird' names of one sort or another: Robin, the oldest, born in the spring; Ossie, six feet, six inches, named after the ostrich; Addie, for Admiral Bird of the South Pole, though Addie is a girl; Dove, the second son, pale and peaceful; Gayle, for nightingale, because she sings; Card, for Cardinal, because he has red hair; Wren, the weakest and tiniest of the Bird family. And lastly, me; Blue, for the Bluebird of Happiness, named for the feeling that overcame my mother the first time she laid eyes on her eighth child . . . or so she told me."

This revelation touched the women in our Group breakout session. One of them, who wore gold bangle bracelets, even got up to retrieve a tissue from her purse. "Oh, isn't that simply—beautiful," she sniffled, her bracelets clinking as she dabbed her eyes.

A few months after Hurricane Dennis slammed into the Florida Panhandle, I told Felicia, "I'm going to leave the county hospital. I've applied for a position with Sacred Heart."

Felicia's expression had turned to stone. "But they don't—they don't . . . make the appropriate legal accommodations for your practice. "

"No, they don't." Uncharacteristic—and wilting— courage. Her white-tipped fingernails chiseled further and further into the prominent bone of her chin as she spoke. "Maybe you're forgetting. *We've* just bought a very large house. We've hired a full time gardener, after a great deal of sifting through applications. Not everyone can be trusted to take care of the plants around the indoor pool. We've made these commitments. Maybe you forgot, since *I'm* the one who had to take care of it all. And then, there's the cook, five days a week." Of course, we rarely ate at home, but she went on. "We owe balances on two cars and pay rent on two offices. I don't think you're thinking clearly. If you go to Sacred Heart, we won't make it." Then she waited for me to respond.

When I didn't, she used a different persuasion, taking my hand, placing it on her breast. "Your idea of what's right is relative. There's no longer an argument for it that can't be quashed. So, are we going to self-destruct because of your silly so-called conscience?" She ran a finger from the tip of my forehead to the buckle on my belt and began what my therapist now calls, 'an impromptu, mutually constructive, sex experience to relieve my misplaced guilt,' Felicia knows sex is my Achilles' heel. Of course she did not *say* that the hoped-for result of her therapy would be my promise not to move to Sacred Heart. But that was the result, with one stipulation on my part: as soon as I made enough money to sustain our lifestyle, I'd redeem myself. And Felicia smiled as if she agreed.

Two years after Dennis, I doubled my income; then two more years passed, but I made no progress toward redemption. Felicia didn't seem to give it a passing thought. I thought of little else—but lacked the spine to say so.

Last September she finally noticed that I was coming apart. To put me back together, she signed me up for Group Therapy.

"Group therapy", she said, "helps men deal with the corrosive issues of childhood that often develop in families such as yours. Trust me. Countless clients have had to turn to it for a time, and it has produced incredible results. I know you're embarrassed, but *I* need you to do it for me, too. If we are going to last. If we are going to get around your fixations."

Felicia went on to say she was glad she hadn't suffered such fixations in her own childhood. She'd never known her father's name, and did just fine without him. Neither did she care much for her mother. "Except that she knew enough to save me from the slavery of—"

Children, I filled in, but the word never made it out.

I pulled away from her; for once, unable to accommodate her touch. A few days later, while she was engrossed in a new harassment case, I made my first trip since the hurricane to The Boat Dock Bar, for my own brand of therapy.

Felicia calls herself a warden of women's rights, and an advocate for a growing file of names, each quickly forgotten after the success of a case. But though she believes otherwise, I know now that she isn't an advocate for me. Beneath her self-espoused title is the subtle cue that all men are a waste of time. Except . . . Felicia likes sex. She likes her job. She likes herself.

I don't like myself. I don't like my job. I *used to* like sex with Felicia, when I thought we were making love. Now, after nearly a decade of marriage, the idea of love confuses me. I don't think I know what it is, and I am sure Felicia doesn't. I don't know whether it ever really existed, or if it was just a big word we gave to much smaller desires.

On the night after the Boat Dock Bar's dissolution, Felicia and I watched the news footage together; watched waves snap pilings like match sticks, the wind shuffle cedar shingles like a deck of cards, and the Gulf swallow what was left. "It's a shame those people died," I said, seeing piece by piece disintegrate. "Why would four sane people stay out on a dock during a hurricane and put their lives in such danger?"

Felicia shrugged. "How do you know they were sane? Maybe they were just plain drunk and had lost all reason. Or maybe they thought they were invincible— they're young, aren't they? And then some people just do crazy things." She picked up a magazine from the glass coffee table. *Beautiful Home*, it was called. She thumbed through until she found the page she was looking for, then showed it to me. "What do you think about redoing our bedroom like the one in this picture— all in red? I'm a little tired of what we have now."

On the TV screen, the mother of one of the young people killed, was sobbing as she was being interviewed. "He was my fourth child. My baby boy. My God, I brought him up with more sense than that!"

"Well, what do you think about the red?" Felicia asked. I left the room.

It only takes fifteen more minutes—two more tequilas for me, and another Coors for the girl across from the table—until we get up to leave for the condo, where she and I will complete the proper procedure, with all of its gyrations, sweat, pulsations and then offer calm, consensual goodbyes. Except, in the pastel light of a vanishing sun, we take a wrong direction; the back way out. We hold to each other, we trip on the steps. We stumble to a stack of rotting wood beside the pilings, and the girl spots what looks to be a small sea gull.

Fishing line is twisted around its torso, squeezing its heart, binding its wings. There's no blood to be seen. It would be worse if there were blood, a visible after-effect of suffering. I see only a plea for mercy in its eyes.

The girl with me sighs, "Poor thing." She bends unsteadily beneath the steps; her bare arms extended, the crest of her breasts exiting her bikini top. Crouched like she is, the string of material between her legs vanishes from view and she looks prehistoric as a woman dressed only in the last rays of sun, and squatting for birth.

She raises the bird to untwist the line, and then coos, "Oh, it isn't a sea gull at all. It's a white dove!" She takes in a breath and closes her eyes in humility, stroking the snow-white feathers as if the bird was a baby she ought to love.

Minutes ago the girl was rubbing the guitar-driven rhythm of her body against me—now a dying bird takes all her attention. What is it in a woman that evokes that reaction—so willing, until some interior searchlight sanctifies a holy connection to life within her? Afterward, some even ask to hold the baby, but it's impossible to re-piece a person from scavenged bits of flesh. Of course, a woman will cry.

The girl with me begins to cry, too. She holds the dove aloft in her hands, looking at me as though I have the power to make it ascend. "You're a doctor. Don't let it die!"

I'm thinking *I don't want it to die! I want it to live.* "I've never saved a bird."

She's annoyed at my reticence. "Drive me to the shelter then. It's only a few blocks away."

Of course, I deliver her. It's my habit to accommodate women by delivery. Spread, cut, scrape, and pay at the desk. She is delivered, and 'it' is erased. Only, at least on the days when I let my guard down, some awful feeling remains, padding the chest like too much cholesterol.

A sun-baked woman opens the screened door to the Destin Wildlife Sanctuary. She has on a heavy, gray sweatshirt imprinted with the logo of an armadillo on a highway, lying on its armored back, its stubby feet straight up like the prongs of a metal comb. Imprinted around the logo is an exclamation: "No More Road Kill!"

The girl with me, whose name I still don't know, hands the dove to the bronze-faced woman. "Is it too late?" The latter puts an arthritic thumb on the bird's breast. "There's no heartbeat. This bird is dead."

The girl gives a primal moan of pain. She's had too much to drink. I've had too much to handle, for what it's cost me.

The woman touches the girl's shoulder, but I believe she's looking at me. "Poor bird. I know how you feel; another victim rashly destroyed." She indicates a sale table of sweatshirts—two for the price of one—same as the one she's wearing. "One of those might help both of you enlighten someone else about this predicament."

She has no idea that a man without spine will never enlighten someone else about any predicament; but there's something good—compassion?—in her claim, so I buy one for each of us.

The intoxicated girl struggles to put hers on. Naturally, I come to her aid, tugging at the shirt until it reaches below the cellulite on her cheeks, covering it completely. She gives me a disenchanted glance, and heads for the Lexus, folding herself into the passenger seat. When I get in, she moves even closer to the window, her despondent eyes on the windshield as if it was a movie screen playing an unhappy ending.

I consider my own intended ending—the condo, with her in my bed. But now, this girl is as far from me as she can get and still be in the car. I take the turn away from the condo, back to The Boat Dock Bar, the only finale either of us really wants in our revised evening calendar.

She gets out, closes the door, and then turns to rest her elbows on the frame of the opened window. Her face turns puzzled, as if she's trying to remember a name she never asked for. "I think you wanted to save it, so it's not your fault."

There's compassion in her voice, but she doesn't wait for my reply. She steps onto the primitive path of crushed oyster shells, walks beneath rows of triangular plastic flags, and takes the reconstructed walkway into the music of aspiring wannabes. Her stride is steady, as if she's suddenly sober.

I return to the condo, sober too.

Steps away from the belly of this stale bedroom is the balcony, and fresh air. The swipe of a white cloud ascends like a wing against the fading, blue sky. Waves splash the beach with a stinging conviction, scouring away the waste of bothersome birds. Caught in the cleansing, I think of Felicia. She expects an accommodation I can no longer give. She will not welcome a different Blue Bird.

I discard my stained Polo, put on the sweatshirt, then make up the bed and collect my things. On my way to the car, I stop by the office to notify the manager—a wizened man in thick glasses—that I intend to sell my condo. "Oh," the manager says, his lips drawn downward. "Haven't you been happy here?"

I give him an unaccommodating reply. "What is happiness?"

The manager thinks a moment, his eyes huge behind his tortoise shell frames. When he finally responds, it's in the tone of a question. "Happiness is when what you believe and what you do are in agreement?"

"Then no," I tell him. "I haven't been happy."

Four hours from Birmingham, the sun slips to darkness and the lights of the Lexus flick on like a beacon, showing the clarified highway ahead. I press the accelerator until I'm flying down the interstate, thankful that this Bird is not dead, but alive, and happier than he's been in years.

Little Things, Big Things

Late at night, after the children are in bed, and she's certain Aaron is sleeping, Amelia takes her flashlight and climbs the back stairs into the attic of the century-old house, to paint. She climbs the wooden steps carefully, barely putting any weight at all on the top step, the one that creaks. In the corner of the attic where the support beam to the rafters makes a perfect right angle with the floor, is a square table with small brass lamp. When she pulls the lamp switch, the table and everything on it, canvas, tubes of oil paint, dry brushes in a glass jar—all come to light in a nearly perfect sphere. She clicks off the flashlight then. A lot of light is neither necessary nor wanted. Tonight she is working on a portrait of Aaron, an eight-by-ten canvas, as all of them are. Portraits of the children are finished, for now anyway; she will come back to them later when she finds a flaw, or when some new characteristic needs to be added. The children's faces, four of them, hang from nails hammered into the pine walls like pictures in a beloved, private gallery. Below, stacked against the wall, are more canvases of each of the children from years past, babyhood onward. But this is the first time she's painted Aaron.

Aaron's unfinished face sits on an easel, looking back at her through deep brown eyes. The eyes are still flat. No highlights yet. Amelia hasn't determined whether the light in his eyes will come from the right, or the left. She pours varnish into a small metal cup, and turpentine into the glass jar, then swishes the brushes around to be sure they are clean, wiping each of them with a stained cotton cloth, pouring out the old, dirtied turpentine, and refilling the jar with the new. On a glass plate, she squeezes out the oil paint, beginning with cadmium yellow light, and titanium white. Highlights for Aaron's eyes. The light will come from the right, she thinks, wondering why she hesitated last night when she began his portrait; the light in each of her portraits always comes from the right, from the only natural light possible in the attic--through one round window that looks like the porthole of a ship. Through that window, occasional moonbeams compete with the lamp, and if the beams are bright enough, as they sometimes are, Amelia turns off the lamp, and paints by moonlight.

Tonight there is no moon, so the lamp stays on. She paints for an hour or so, until Aaron's face is just like she wants it, charged with an expression of love and faithfulness accented by the meticulous highlights in his eyes. Then she takes the canvas and hangs it on a waiting nail, beside the portrait of their last child, Aaron Junior. She cleans off the brushes again, closes the paint tubes, and steps over to the round window in order to look out into the darkness, where a few stars wink back at her. Turning off the small lamp, she clicks on the flashlight and proceeds down the stairs, one at a time, until, reaching the second story of her old house, she snuggles in bed beside Aaron. Sleeps comes easily as she releases a breath of satisfaction and equilibrium.

The second floor bedroom, hers and Aaron's, is in the shape of a perfect square. There is an imposing rectangular, glassed window on the east side, beginning at the ceiling, ending at the heart pine floor. Mornings, when the sun is shining and the white chiffon curtains are drawn back, a ray of lemon yellow light will brush over the white damask spread, and splash a perfect, pale triangle over the finely chiseled petals of wooden roses on their mahogany headboard. The room and the light are balanced. They relate to each other, just as they should, just as she and Aaron do. *Don't we?* she asks herself, startling from sleep. All seems proportional then, and stable. Unless Aaron gets out of their bed and raises the daunting window, letting the chiffon blow over her face like an unruly dress. Then shadows disturb the stability of light, and sounds of rumbling waves rush in like a trespasser, and Amelia senses disorder. But this morning when she awakens, Aaron isn't beside her. He's gone, she supposes, to do the job he always does on Saturdays.

Today is overcast. The white sand is less white, no pyramid of light floods the room. *A lack,* she tells herself. *Lack of symmetry.* She won't attempt to pull back the sheer curtains, and certainly won't raise the glassed window. She simply looks through them, to observe the beach below.

The lime green Gulf appears calm. An unfamiliar man with a net is walking into the frothing waves to scoop up crabs with blue-tipped claws; big crabs, the size of his large hand. The crabs try to escape into deeper water, but the man seems much too experienced, and his bucket is nearly full. *Mayhem is in the making,* Amelia thinks, watching the capture, and recalling Aaron's own filled bucket at dusk the afternoon before. "Get out the stock pot, wife," he called to her, apparently pleased to see her waiting on the porch.

She was used to cooking live crabs, but she cringed each time—their shells clacking and claws clicking inside the large, metal pot on the stove, until the simmering, slow boil finally kills them. She'd heard you could put crabs in the freezer before cooking them, to stun them a bit. That sounded more humane to Amelia, but Aaron wouldn't hear of it. "Stupid," he called it. "They're only crabs." So she cooked them the way she always cooked them. Then she sat at the table to eat with Aaron and the children; all of them cracking the claws, one against the other, and then prying off the main shell to eat the rest of the meat with their fingers.

As usual, she'd warned the children. "Pull away the dead man's fingers. Never eat the gills of a crab." And when Aaron, Jr., grinned at his mother, dug out the feathery looking structure and put it to his lips in jest; Amelia practically shouted, "It's not a silly joke Aaron Junior. The dead man's fingers are dangerous. Death is a big thing!"

"But I'm not going to die from eating them. The fingers just taste bad that's all."

"Then why in the world would you want to put them into your mouth? That's all out of proportion and makes no sense at all. You *must* learn to balance your thinking, especially if you're going to be a musician."

Of course, she doesn't know whether he'll be a musician or not. He's young and only just starting piano and violin. But he is creative, like her. Already, he sees how one thing relates to another. Maybe soon, he'll be conscious of the way chord progressions and musical phrases become a perfect cadence, just as she is keen to the way various shapes meld with a multitude of colors when she completes an image on canvas. Always, she paints the image the way *she* wants to see it, the way *she* relates to something, or someone. Take a circle, for instance. To her, a circle is endless, something perfect. Its perfection signifies a harmony destined to last. Anytime she paints that shape she is driven to do so by her unquenchable desire for perfection. Other shapes and colors work similarly in her mind, mostly unbeknownst to her, though from time to time she feels this manner of thinking straining at her brain. But she keeps all this within. She doesn't speak about it, not even to Aaron.

"Oh, leave the boy alone," Aaron had said. And so, she had.

Now, Aaron passes behind her in the bedroom. "I'm all done," he says. He has finished mowing the circle of green grass around the old house--his personal conquest of the sand which, if not for the sturdy barrier of green, would extend up to the porch. Years ago, he planted the small, round lawn after some dinner guests had commented on the dryness, the dullness of so much sand, and he has nurtured it every Saturday since, keeping it clipped and perfectly ring-shaped. The circle of green is one big thing that's important to both of them.

He enters the bathroom to wash up, and she follows him. From the medicine cabinet, he takes out a box of sodium bicarbonate, pouring some into a glass of water and stirring it with a spoon he also keeps in the cabinet. The clicking and clacking of the spoon against the glass reminds her of the crabs in the metal pot, which takes her to the *Dead Man's Fingers*, and then to death itself.

"If you were to die tomorrow, Aaron"—an impromptu question—"would you be proud of the things you've done?"

He splashes water over his face. "Define proud." Aaron likes definition, but in the beveled mirror, his face is blurred by spattering water, laced with sand.

Amelia comes closer. "At peace with yourself."

"Maybe I'd be proud," Aaron says, "but I'm not planning to die tomorrow."

"Nobody knows when they will die."

"Oh?" Aaron smiles; a familiar smile, one he uses after a defining decision to make love. Amelia picks a blade of grass from the sleeve of his T-shirt. He turns to touch her cheek, just as the telephone rings.

"I'll get it, Mom!" Beth Anne's voice comes from her bedroom down the hall, but Amelia answers first. Her shoulders tighten when she hears and registers who it is.

"He can't come to the phone right now, Claudine," she says. "If there's a problem at the office, then call someone who knows how to fix it. Someone besides Aaron." She hears an irate suck of breath, and then, Claudine's terse words, "Listen, Amelia, you need to . . ."

Aaron takes the phone, cradling the receiver between his chin and shoulder. "Claudine?"

"Wait, I'd like to know what she thinks I need to do," Amelia says with a hand on his forearm, indicating that he should hand back the phone.

Aaron covers the receiver with his hand. "You need to do nothing. It's just the fax machine. I know how to fix it."

Amelia gives a futile sign. She doubts he knows how to fix anything, except the grass circle. Still, Claudine is such a pain, so much trouble for Aaron. She doesn't like the woman, though she hasn't said so to Aaron; and she's certain Claudine doesn't like her. On her way out of the room, she pictures Claudine as Medusa, with her long--and stringy--golden hair flying about her face, until each tuft is turned into a writhing black snake. But she discards the image of Claudine when she passes Beth Anne's room, seeing her own golden-haired child curled like a gentle kitten on her bed, fallen back to sleep with a book in her hands. She won't allow any shapeless Medusa to disturb that sweet picture of harmony—though she realizes that by the time she wakes, Beth Anne, being the teenager she is, might shake up her mother's present, pretty vision.

After he showers, Aaron leaves for the insurance office where he works. Amelia doesn't question his departure, which has become a habit of little concern; or why Claudine is at the office on a Saturday at all. No woman so out-of-shape, and with such a mannishly aggressive personality, could ever be a threat to Amelia. Besides, she no longer questions little things; only big things, like how a person should live in order to die proud.

Once, soon after their marriage, Aaron climbed inside their ground-level apartment through the bedroom window. It was midnight and he couldn't find his key. Amelia doesn't like out-of-line behavior, and she despises confrontation, but she lit into him that night because he smelled like a brewery.

"You shouldn't have locked the door!" he shouted, as if his mistake was hers. "The office party lasted longer than I expected, and I only had a couple of drinks." He stumbled to the bathroom, heaving, and Amelia mopped his head with a cold towel.

"You'd never lie to me, would you Aaron?" she asked, leading him to bed.

"You're supposed to trust your husband. Quit picking on me about every little thing." Then he had opened an eye. "I love you, Amelia."

The incident kept Amelia up until dawn. While Aaron slept, she went over all possibilities of why he might be late, and drunk; then discounted every one of them. She'd known Aaron all her life. For a while he had guarded her like a big brother; and later, when she fell in love with him, she saw him as a perfect circle, a fence around her, protecting her from all that was imperfect in the world. When she turned eighteen, he asked her to marry him. He said he loved her, and she believed he did. Never before had he given her a reason to mistrust him. So, sitting beside him on the bed that night, stroking his face, feeling his breath on her hands, she decided to ignore the little things and concentrate on the big ones.

For Amelia, family is the biggest thing. She sees herself as one of fewer and fewer women who put husband and children above career. "I just don't understand why there are so few stay-at-home moms," she says to Allie, one of a few friends who stays home full time too, "I don't know how a woman could do anything else." And Allie, who affirms everything she says, adds, "It's up to us, Amelia. I mean, at the very least we're picking up slack for so many women who . . ."

Amelia is a Brownie leader who makes fires and teaches survival skills. She is a home-room mother who carries out Valentine parties and carves herself into the minds of teachers handing out grades, inviting them to her annual afternoon tea of cucumber sandwiches, homemade cheese straws, and sugared pecans. She works on her parish council to be certain her children's school receives an ample percentage of the church's Sunday collections, and she cautiously surveys the politics of the ever-slippery city council, which can be kept from sliding under the table if policed closely enough by the handful of women, like Amelia, who know what the *big things* are. If she doesn't do it, who will?

She's proud of her family. In addition to the portraits she paints of them, she hangs her children's art on the refrigerator alongside the many newspaper clippings about Aaron. When the stories fade, she puts up new ones, saving the old ones in a red heart-shaped box. The heart box was once filled with chocolate candy from Aaron. He had attached a note. "With all my love," it read. That he loves her is all Amelia needs to hear to keep going.

Last year, Aaron Fuller became The Executive Vice-President of Crescent Insurance Company. A decisive man, and good-looking, Aaron is mostly there when Amelia needs him, and well-represented in her heart box of treasured things. Pictures of him as Chamber of Commerce President, United Way Chairman, School-board Representative, even Boss of the Year.

Amelia sees Aaron as an executive father, too. Executive father. That's what she lovingly calls him to his face, and behind his back; one is the same as the other to Amelia. Her favorite picture is of Aaron sitting on their bed, holding their first child, Beth Anne, against his bare chest. Whenever Amelia sees it, she wants to make love to Aaron, then and there.

Beth Anne is now fifteen: tall, like Aaron, and with the same occasional streak of unpredictability that throws things off balance for Amelia. Beth Anne causes her many sleepless nights; still, Amelia sees her graduating at the top of her class, if she can keep her daughter out of trouble. Their second daughter, Starla, has assumed the look of a yellow-haired pop star, though she's a little overweight. But it's temporary; when Amelia was thirteen, she gained weight, too, and then lost it. Besides, Starla is a kind-hearted girl, with the highest average in the Junior High Beta Club. Their son, Aaron Junior, is not as school-smart as his sisters, but his creative talents make up for that—piano, Suzuki violin, and who knows what's next for him? Their youngest, Kathleen, has copper-colored hair like Amelia's. She is both smart and talented. Today, the refrigerator is covered with Kathleen's drawings.

The week goes by as usual for the Fullers; Aaron tending to insurance, Amelia tending to her family. On Friday afternoon, Amelia is back from a Teacher's Appreciation Tea that she and her friends have given at their children's school. She has taken Deidre home. The house is sparkling; Deidre has done a good job, as usual.

Amelia is looking forward to Aaron's office party tonight, and to the fact that tomorrow is Saturday, and Aaron will be home. He will work in the yard again, because he likes to do that; but he will probably go to the office for a while, too. Aaron wants the Board of Directors to elect him President. He wants to make his family proud, so he has to sacrifice a bit. "If I don't go the extra mile," he says, "I may as well call it quits now." Amelia wants what Aaron wants. His weekend work at

153

the office is annoying, but it's a little thing. She won't nag him about it.

She notices the clock against the daisy wallpaper of the kitchen. It is the third week of a new school year for her children. She has fifteen minutes before she needs to pick them up from Our Lady of Sorrows. Already she can hear the release bell ringing. The drive takes only five minutes, so she changes into jeans and a white cotton sweater. When Aaron comes home, she hopes he will notice how nicely the jeans fit her, and then, after he notices her figure, she will change into a special dress, the one she will wear to the party.

A few weeks ago, Aaron pointed out the dress on the dog-eared page of a catalog he came home with. He asked why she never wore anything like it, the backless, black velvet dress, the front bodice studded with rhinestones. She could have asked him how a busy man has time to thumb through women's catalogs, but that was such a little thing to worry about. It probably belonged to one of the girls in the office, and may have been left on a table in the food lounge where he could have picked it up, and then seeing the dress, thought Amelia would like it. In fact, she didn't like it, but she ordered the dress in order to please. Tonight, she will wear it for Aaron.

Because it is a party night, she will order pizza for the children's supper; they love pizza from The Dough Tosser. Beth Anne will not be home; she's spending the evening with her best friend, Amy. Of course, Amelia will check to be sure Beth Anne is there, and then Starla will babysit Aaron Junior and Kathleen. The plans are made.

On her way to Our Lady of Sorrows, Amelia stops the car to examine the crack in the foundation of their house. She noticed it nearly a year ago, and at first, the sight of it nearly stopped her heart. This was their house, their happy home. The crack smacked her across the face. But then she regrouped. It really wasn't a big crack. Lots of old houses have cracks in them and their owners don't appear that concerned. So, though it bothered Amelia, she decided to ignore it, to brush it aside as one more little thing. She decided to see her house, like she did most things, just as she wanted to see it: whole, balanced, and proportional, a place in which her family related to each other as they should. So she'd said nothing to Aaron.

Then, last week Aaron noticed the divide in the stonework. "Hell! If we don't get that goddamned thing fixed, the freaking house will fall down." Amelia, who was working in the garden with Kathleen, put her hands over the child's ears and accidentally flicked sand into her eyes. She had to carry the screaming child into the house to wash it out, but calming Kathleen was more important than the crack. Looking at it now, she still doesn't see a big crack, only a small one. A bit of mortar will fix it just fine. She makes a mental note to call someone who knows about foundations, someone besides Aaron.

The sandy road that leads to the rear of the Fuller house is a narrow one. A car coming from the opposite direction has to pull off into a neighbor's yard, often

Jenna's yard. Jenna works at the insurance company where Aaron works. 'The Office Talk-Show Host," he calls her. "Don't believe a word that woman says," Aaron has told Amelia, often enough.

A couple of weeks ago, when Amelia pulled onto Jenna's grass to allow for a coming car, Jenna came running from her house, waving, signaling for Amelia to stop and talk. Jenna said she'd learned something Amelia might be interested in. "I don't have time to talk now," Amelia said. "I have to pick up the children."

Now, she drives down the narrow road. Again, Jenna waves her over, and again Amelia gives the same excuse. Little things, and little people like Jenna, complicate the bigger things in life. Aaron would surely agree with her about that.

At Our Lady of Sorrows School, the children, minus Beth Anne, pile in. Kathleen proudly hands her mother a crayon etching of Christ on the Cross. Amelia studies the heart. She notices the fracture in its red center and the penciled water pouring from the side of the Savior.

"That's the sign of mercy," Kathleen says, pointing to the water. "Sister Mary said I drew it just right."

"Yes. Just right," Amelia agrees.

Then Kathleen begins to sing, "*There's a wideness in God's mercy, like the wideness of the sea.*"

"Oh, not again," Starla grumbles from the back seat. "We practiced singing that all afternoon in assembly, and I'm tired of it!" Kathleen stops singing immediately. Her eyes fill with tears.

Amelia gives Starla a reprimanding look in the rear-view mirror, and at once, Starla hugs her sister. "Mother will put your etching on the refrigerator as soon as we get home," Starla tells Kathleen. "And you can sing if you want to." Amelia smiles at both of them.

Aaron's car is parked just outside the garage. "Why's Daddy home so early? Aaron Junior asks.

"Get off my new purse, nerd!" Starla stomps her brother's foot and yanks her new purse from beneath Aaron Junior's thigh. Amelia sighs, thinking that at thirteen, kind-heartedness comes and goes.

"Ow, you big hippo!" Aaron Junior yells.

"Mom, I don't want to baby sit that creep," Starla whines. "Why can't I spend the night with a friend like Beth Anne? It's not fair!" Then the telephone rings inside and Starla races to answer it.

"Mommy, if she spends the night out, can I have a friend over, too?" Kathleen asks.

"Starla's not spending the night out, sugar. She's babysitting you and Aaron, Jr. The plans are made, and Starla knows that."

Aaron Junior inspects the interior of his father's car. "Daddy left his suit coat," he says suspiciously, as if the neglect was a clue. "Why did you say he was home so early?" Aaron Junior has changed his mind about being a musician. He wants to be a trial lawyer when he grows up. That's alright with Amelia; she supposes Aaron Junior will see many proportional connections in that, too.

"Probably to get ready for the party," Amelia says to her son, though it never takes Aaron more than a few minutes to get ready for anything.

"Maybe he's got a surprise for us. I'll bet we're getting the puppy!" Kathleen squeals, and hurries inside.

Aaron Junior follows his sisters. "Don't you dare order the pizza!" he yells to them. "It's my turn to call Dough Tossers." The door slams behind him.

The children race up the stairs into the kitchen where they will take out cereal or ice cream or cookies and juice, making a multitude of crumbs and dairy-fresh stains on the Deidre-shined mahogany table. Amelia takes a breath and reaches into Aaron's car for his suit coat. On the floor of the back seat, there is a small bag of ready-mix concrete. She smiles at Aaron's obvious intention to repair the fracture in the foundation of their house, but she knows the sack will only end up on a garage shelf. She carries his coat into the house, along with Kathleen's etching.

On the stairs, Kathleen is talking to her father. "Can we get the puppy for Easter?"

"We'll see." Aaron says, smoothing her copper-colored hair.

"I love you, Daddy," Kathleen says.

Amelia follows Aaron to their bedroom, past the table covered with book bags. She closes the door to the noise of opening cabinets, the clinking of spoons, the rustling of cookie bags, and the voices of children. In their bedroom, she says, "You are home a little early." She lays his coat and Kathleen's etching on the end of their bed, and catches a whiff of the expensive cologne she gave Aaron for Father's Day. She wants to put her arms around him, but there is a worrisome look on his face.

"Before we go to the party, I thought I'd try to fix that damn split in the house," he says.

"Oh, I don't think it's a big thing, honey." Amelia wants to let him off the hook; she knows from his voice he doesn't think he can handle the fixing. She touches his neck. She wants him to say how nice she looks in the jeans. He doesn't.

"That crack needs to be fixed, Amelia."

"I'll call a construction company to come out and look at it next week."

"Okay. It's your decision." More and more Aaron is happy to pass responsibility to her.

Aaron Junior orders the pizza, and Amelia and Aaron get dressed for the party. They stand side by side in front of the beveled mirror. Amelia puts in the diamond studs Aaron gave her for Christmas, and he smiles when she reminds him of that. He doesn't appear to notice the dress she is wearing, the ordered dress from the catalog he brought home.

On the way to the Country Club, she tells him, "Don't drink too much tonight."

"Don't make it such a big thing!" he says, using her language, her constant categorization of everything into little things, big things. Then he touches her hand as if he's sorry he snapped at her. She sloughs off the remark and he changes the subject. "Did you hear about tonight's predicted meteor shower? It should happen about the time the party's over."

"Then we'll have to watch it," she says, enjoying the warmth of his hand on hers.

The falling stars are the topic of conversation at the party and the subject of Aaron's many toasts. When Amelia finally reaches for his glass, he drunkenly shoves against her, splashing bourbon over her arm. He leans close to her ear as if to kiss her, instead he slurs, "I've heard a meteor shower predicts the end of an era." Only then does he appear to notice, with surprise, the black velvet dress she is wearing.

At the same moment, there is a polite tap from behind, on Amelia's bare shoulder. "Don't panic," a familiar voice says, "but we're in the same outfit." She turns to face a gleeful Claudine. That shapeless Medusa with a hideous face, snakes in her hair, and a look that turns a victim to stone, is smiling back at her with a *gotcha* look. "Aaron showed it to me in the catalog," Claudine goes on as if she can't wait to explain. "He told me," she pauses, takes a deep breath, and deliberates, "told me not to take it the wrong way, but that it would be a reward for all my hard work in the office, if I liked it. Of course, I loved it!" Aaron is standing between them with a petrified expression. Claudine gives him a quick, vexed glance, as though accusing him of an inexcusable degree of stupidity. "But he never said he was ordering one for you, too, Amelia."

Amelia is used to justifications, excuses from Aaron. Aaron can make everything sound reasonable . . . but not

Claudine. There is *nothing* reasonable, *nothing* little about Aaron giving her a dress, especially not *this* dress. The situation calls for a proportional response.

"But Claudine, are you sure we're in the same dress?" Amelia looks her up and down. "If we are, no one will recognize it. That dress certainly doesn't look the same *on you* as it does on me."

Claudine appears as insulted as Amelia meant her to be.

Aaron's frozen lips quickly defrost into a Cheshire cat grin. "You little witch." He slings an arm around her shoulders, pulling her toward him as if she's made him proud. "How about you and your broom come to the other side of the room?" She walks with him, his arm heavier with each step. They stop at a table of hors d'oeuvres, but before she can get an honest answer from him about the dress, he leaves to make another trip to the bar.

Answers come a little later, with Aaron's drunken reflection in a gilded mirror behind her. Amelia turns to see the real picture. He's running a finger down Claudine's bare back, around the twin seams of black velvet. Maybe he's high enough to confuse his secretary with his wife, but Amelia is worn out with excuses. She leaves the party, less from humiliation than from an unfamiliar stab of anger that completely destroys her equilibrium. Leaves a long crack in her invented world. Driving home, a forgotten truth about Medusas surges to the surface: the reason the hideous woman was stricken with ugliness in the first place. It was plain sex,

161

performed in the temple of a goddess, with a man who was thought to be trustworthy.

It's two thirty when Aaron flops into bed beside her, reeking of Seagram's. "Too bad about the dress," he drawls, as if that was all there was to it, such a little thing.

Amelia doesn't ask who delivered him home; he falls asleep too quickly. She leaves the bed, and heaving the last of her strength upon the glassed rectangular window, raises it. The chiffon curtains blow back, over her face, but she seizes the flimsy material and wrestles it into the window hooks. The sound of the waves assaults the room like a destructive thief after something precious, while the wind twists her copper hair into coils. Still, she remains within the frame of the window, facing the disorder, and the black sky beyond.

At once, a tiny star bursts into brilliance above the dark water, scattering hundreds of sapphires that cascade in neon treks, like loosely sewn rhinestones tumbling from a black velvet dress. Aaron's snores chug train-like behind her, while the explosions of light illuminate her thoughts. Claudine and Aaron, *right in front of her face!*

A week passes, maybe two. Aaron seems to have forgotten about the party, about the dress, even about Claudine—at least, she hasn't called the house. As she always does, Amelia nightly climbs the stairs to the attic, where the portrait of Aaron has been taken from the wall and set back on the easel—for touch-ups. She turns on the lamp, arranges the oils and brushes, and readies herself, but she hasn't laid down one stroke. To do so

162

she would need to erase his expression of love, faithfulness, and the meticulous highlights in his eyes; it would erase what she, the artist, has created. Downstairs, Kathleen's etching of Christ on the cross still hangs on the refrigerator. Beth Anne is becoming more rebellious, Starla has gained at least five more pounds, and Aaron Junior has decided he doesn't want to be a trial lawyer anymore. She can't just give up; the children matter. Something must be done about all those big things. And then, Aaron corners her in the bedroom.

"Your friend, Claudine," he begins, in the familiar tone he uses to disseminate responsibility.

"My friend?"

"You're the one who asked me to hire her."

"I only told her about the opening. You hired her."

"Well, I shouldn't have."

He sits on the bed. She sits beside him. "What is it, Aaron?"

There are tears in his eyes. "I—I got the axe. The company made me resign."

"*Oh* Aaron, why?" She asks this with heart-felt compassion for the lost boy within him, once beloved as a brother, and despite what she suspects, someone she still loves.

"Apparently, Claudine called some damn employee helpline a few weeks ago to say I was harassing her, and the board got wind of it. I told them it was a little thing, that she was just a disgruntled employee who hadn't gotten a big enough raise. They said if I apologized to her I'd probably get only a slap on the wrist, a reprimand. But it didn't go that way."

"A reprimand for what?"

He turns his face toward the window. "I kissed her-- just once, in the office, but it wasn't harassment. She came after me. You know yourself how many times she's called the house."

"You kissed her?"

"She called me into a supply closet, to show me something, and then-- It wasn't me; it was her!"

"But she wouldn't have kissed you just out of the blue, Aaron, unless you'd given some encouragement."

"I'm sorry, baby." He hasn't called her 'baby' for years. He reaches for her, just as Kathleen opens the door.

"Mama, can I call Tiffany to sleep over?"

Amelia tries to speak normally. "This is not a good weekend, sugar."

"But yesterday, you said I could."

"Kathleen, your mother and I are talking," Aaron says firmly. Kathleen knows to leave the room.

"I'll find a better job, Amelia," Aaron continues. "I'm not on the beach for good."

The only word that stuck in her mind was 'beach.' As a child, she'd stood on the wide edge of the gulf as the tide pulled sand from under her feet. It was a game she played with herself to see how long she could keep balanced, but the little hole she stood in grew bigger and bigger. In the end, the sucking water always won.

"More than likely I can move over to Crescent Insurance. I probably won't even miss a paycheck." Aaron is still sitting beside her on the edge of their bed. "Really Amelia, it was just a kiss, such a little thing." This time she scents his deception, the way he has turned her categories into a knife to the throat.

She goes into the bathroom and locks the door. When he tries to open it, she kicks it, as if she is kicking Aaron. "It is not a little thing!"

By Friday, Aaron has another job. He made some phone calls, pulled some strings. He's even made sure that the Friday paper boasts his picture. The caption reads: "Popular Executive Moves to Crescent Insurance." Amelia does not clip it out.

Through the kitchen window, she watches a Sea Hawk circling the beach; a black-masked bird with a piercing golden eye, its wing-span enormous as it sails on currents of air. It scans the shallow part of the water, inches from the surface, searching for prey. In perfect ellipses, it rises, rolls, and swoops downward again, skimming the Gulf's edge, then up, down, and around once more. For quite a while she waits for the hawk to dive and be victorious, to complete the cycle she's seen so many times before. Then, all at once, it plunges into the water, feet first, talons spread, its wings held up and back for the powerful stroke it will take to raise its prey.

Except it can't rise; the fish is too big. And it can't let go; its talons are embedded in the fish's flesh. All the bird can do is thrash about, defeated.

She turns from the window, looking for anything to distract her from watching the bird drown.

Friday is Deidre's day off, so Amelia straightens the house. She takes a roast from the freezer for dinner, then makes two phone calls; one, to cancel a luncheon invitation, the other to cancel Aaron Junior's Suzuki lesson. Finally, she turns on the television. She flips through the channels until she comes to a court room drama. She could have been a judge. Her father always encouraged her to go to law school, start with small things—petty cases of civil suits. And then go on to the big thing: to preside as judge over the very law itself. In this show the judge stays steel eyed while the defendant sweats so profusely that even the faraway cameras pick up stains under his armpits.

Aaron sweats, too, when she finally gets the truth out of him. He is standing in front of the refrigerator, profiled against the crayon etching of Christ on the cross, confessing, "Alright, it wasn't just a kiss. But if you'd paid me more attention, maybe it wouldn't have happened."

Amelia turns for their bedroom, opens the walk-in closet, steps on a stool to reach the top drawer, and lifts out the heart-shaped box filled with treasured things. She separates the many yellowed clippings about Aaron and crumples them into a paper ball. The clump is so large that when she flushes it down the toilet it clogs the plumbing, clogs every bit of plumbing.

Outside, water pours from the expanding fissure in the foundation of their house—a very big thing. And neither Aaron nor Amelia knows how to fix it.

Jimmy's Cat

Jimmy's cat wasn't born one-eyed. I heard he lost it one night in a heat-fight with a big, orange-striped tom when Jimmy was twelve years old. Jimmy's twenty-seven, now, and the vet who sewed up the cat's eye, sewed it so tight it looks like it was never meant to see in the first place.

Jimmy's cat didn't have a real name. Everybody just called it *Jimmy's Cat*. Jimmy's mama called it Jimmy's Cat. Jimmy's grandmamma called it Jimmy's Cat. And Jimmy's wife, when he got married, called it Jimmy's Cat, too.

Jimmy's mama and grandmamma never cared too much for Jimmy's Cat. Jimmy's mama didn't like when it would creep out of Jimmy's bed in the mornings and into the kitchen, rubbing itself up against her leg while she was pouring the beat eggs into the frying pan. She'd get a scrunched-up look on her face whenever it would butt the blind side of its head to her calf like it was trying to push her out. The little, brown mole on the side of her cheek would quiver whenever Jimmy's cat did that. And when it slid around her ankle, like a fuzzy rope trying to snag her, she'd clinch her front teeth, and curl up her lips, and just about have a hissy fit. Because Jimmy's mama didn't allow herself to be tied to nobody, at least nobody but Jimmy. So, if Jimmy wasn't in the kitchen, she'd take the broom to Jimmy's Cat and swat it outside.

Jimmy's grandmamma didn't find Jimmy's Cat tolerable, either, because it liked to sleep between the tire and the fender of her car—only her car, nobody else's— not even Jimmy's wife's old jalopy. So Jimmy's grandmamma always checked under the fender before she got in to drive it. Then she checked the inside of the car, because there was no doubt some redneck maniac might be hiding in the back seat waiting to do God-knows-what to her. Finally, she'd check the tires, because one time she had a flat one smack dab in the middle of the Interstate, and had to catch a ride to the nearest filling station with a sweaty, fat man who almost talked her ear off. She said she never in her life wanted to go through an ordeal like that again, so she made it a habit to inspect the car, inside and out, before each errand and departure. And sometimes she had to scoot off Jimmy's Cat, curled up on top of the right front wheel under the fender where nobody could have seen it, not even somebody with good eyes.

Although Jimmy's mama and Jimmy's grandmamma didn't give a hoot for Jimmy's Cat, they both cared an awful lot about Jimmy. Jimmy's mama was always saying how he'd been the best little old football player in the Rangertown Recreation League, and if anybody made a grunt that sounded to her like they were half-way impressed, she'd move in closer on them, sharpen up her eyes, and tell the story about how Jimmy had gone to the state finals. Then, right about the time she was as in their face as she could possibly get without kissing 'em, she'd tell them that, when he was in high school, her Jimmy had won the Most Valuable Player award in at least six games. Jimmy's mama was in her twentieth year of pressing up to people with her stories, so just about everybody in Rangertown had heard them at least once. But during the year they'd been married, Jimmy's wife had heard the stories more than anybody. She could have told them all from memory if she wanted to. But she didn't.

Jimmy's grandmamma paid all kinds of attention to Jimmy's needs like she was the only one who could keep him happy. She was always saying, "Jimmy, are you sure you don't need me to fix you some more chocolate pie, or boiled custard?" or whatever else she could do for him anytime of the day. She especially liked to pay attention to Jimmy while he was paying attention to his cat.

One night Jimmy was sitting in the swing on the front porch and Jimmy's Cat was curled up in his lap. It was the very night Jimmy asked his wife (who of course wasn't Jimmy's wife at the time on account of they hadn't had a wedding yet) to marry him, and she was just fixing to say yes, when Jimmy's grandmamma decided to come out from behind the curtained window where Jimmy's wife had a suspicion she'd been hiding all along. Jimmy's grandmamma grabbed onto the swing where Jimmy and Jimmy's Cat and Jimmy's wife were all enjoying each other and hollered—loud enough to beat the band—that she was having a first-rate heart attack. Then she fell right into Jimmy's lap, which meant Jimmy's Cat, noticeably annoyed, had to squeeze itself out from under her and run for its very life.

Soon as Jimmy's mama heard all the commotion, she came scrambling out onto the porch, too, and told Jimmy's wife to go call the doctor—which she did, right off. And even though the doctor said directly to Jimmy's grandmamma's face that she hadn't had nothing but a little gas, Jimmy's grandmamma just sighed and said, "Well, I guess I just have to get used to being a heart patient."

The very next day Jimmy up and married his wife right out of the blue, without asking Jimmy's mama or Jimmy's grandmamma down to the Justice of the Peace to watch. After that, both of them started asking Jimmy, "Jimmy, you sure that wife of yours is treating you right?" Jimmy's mama and grandmamma were like that. Always.

After Jimmy got married, they seemed to start caring a lot more about Jimmy's Cat, usually in front of Jimmy's wife. One of them would pick it up and stroke it and then say, "Jimmy don't love another thing in this world much as he loves this cat." And while Jimmy's Cat hissed and dug its claws into her arm, the other would look over at Jimmy's wife to be sure she was listening, and say, "Yes ma'am, you are surely correct." Then they'd talk about when Jimmy was ten or eleven years old and he used to take the cat with him to the picture show to watch Dewayne "The Rock" Johnson in the movies. Dewayne used to be a football star, too; that's why Jimmy liked his movies so much. And they'd tell Jimmy's wife about how Jimmy would be way down the block from the ticket window and hide the cat underneath his football jacket because he didn't want to be parted from what he'd grown up with. Jimmy's mama would say she guessed Jimmy's Cat knew to just sit there and not make any noises so Jimmy wouldn't get thrown out of the picture show. Then Jimmy's grandmamma would say to Jimmy's wife again, "Wasn't it something how Jimmy loved that cat more than anything else in this whole wide world?"

The fact is, Jimmy's wife knew it was true about him loving his cat so much, because he let it in their bed every night with his own pretty face squared up right next to the sewed-up eye. Jimmy's wife didn't say much about the cat sleeping in between them because of all the times Jimmy's mama and Jimmy's grandmamma had told her how Jimmy was already attached to something besides her. She just steeled herself and said, sometimes in a whisper so quiet that only she could hear, "Might as well accept it." And anyway, since Jimmy and Jimmy's wife had to live with Jimmy's mama and grandmamma because Jimmy hadn't found another job, Jimmy's wife felt like the house was beyond her wants, that the cat was there before she was; so she reckoned it could sleep wherever it wanted. And one more reason. Since Jimmy's wife loved Jimmy, she thought she ought to love his cat, so she tried to.

Jimmy did have a job, at least when he first got married. He worked for the city, hauling off debris and such like that. But, pretty soon, Jimmy quit. Jimmy's mama said he was too smart to be picking up trash anyway, and Jimmy's grandmamma said he ought to be in a managerial position since he was very good at running things. Jimmy's wife wondered, "*What things?*"

But she only wondered that once and no more because the one time she mentioned it, Jimmy's grandmamma gave her an ugly look and said she guessed she knew Jimmy better than her daughter-in-law. So Jimmy's wife got her own job, nine to five, hauling groceries at the Winn Dixie store on Highway 52 where Jimmy's mama and Jimmy's grandmamma shopped.

At the store, she got to know some of the check-out girls pretty well. The girls always asked about Jimmy because they remembered him from high school. One day, even the manager came up to the check-out counter where Jimmy's wife was packing up groceries and said he hadn't realized she was Jimmy's wife until then. He said he used to watch Jimmy play football for the Rangertown High Bobcats and that in all his years of sitting in the Rangertown stadium, he had honestly never seen a better running back than Jimmy had been, and she must be proud to be Jimmy's wife. Jimmy's wife said she was, said it loud because the girls at the check-out were listening. Then the manager said to tell Jimmy to come in sometime so he could meet him. Jimmy's wife said okay, she would.

Jimmy's wife had two half-way good eyes, but she needed glasses to see when she read. She always did like to read so she asked the manager if she could have all the out-of-date tabloids that hadn't sold and he said, "Anything for Jimmy's wife!"

She took the tabloids home and that night in bed, on the other side of Jimmy's Cat, she propped up on her pillow to read every printed word. But when Jimmy's mama and Jimmy's grandmamma came into Jimmy's bedroom, like they did each night at ten o'clock to kiss him goodnight, they saw Jimmy's wife reading with her glasses on, and started calling her 'owl face.' Pretty soon, Jimmy said he didn't like the way she looked in her glasses anymore, so Jimmy's wife tried to read without them.

One night Jimmy's wife put down her tabloid magazine—she couldn't really read without her glasses, and, without captions, some of the pictures were downright overwhelming—and reached over the cat to poke Jimmy awake. She asked him what he thought about them (she and Jimmy's Cat and Jimmy) moving to their own place. She said she thought the manager at Winn Dixie would give Jimmy a job because the manager admired him, too. Jimmy seemed interested and asked if that meant he could be in charge of the meat department. Jimmy's wife squinted at him, since her eyes had to adjust from reading without her glasses to seeing a person, and said, "Well maybe," in a tone that made *maybe* seem like *yes*, though she hadn't the slightest idea in the world.

Jimmy put his arm around the neck of his cat and hugged it. "Okay then," he said, "I'll go see the manager tomorrow."

The next morning, Jimmy put on his old football jacket and rode to work with Jimmy's wife. Jimmy's wife asked him didn't he think it was too warm for a coat and shouldn't he just leave it in her car? Jimmy said he guessed she was right, so he took it off carefully, gave it a hug and laid it on the back seat. Jimmy's wife went on into the store.

In the store, Jimmy's wife motioned to the manager to come up to the check-out counter to meet Jimmy, who was just coming through the swinging door. She felt kind of proud looking at Jimmy because the check-out girls were looking at him, too, like they wished he was married to them.

Jimmy and the manager were standing too far away from where Jimmy's wife was packing groceries for her to hear what all they were saying, but she saw Jimmy explaining the way he used to catch a pass. She knew that's what he was doing because Jimmy began to take little short, hopping steps backwards, cradling the air like there was something in his arms. Then she saw the manager's face go from interest to anger when Jimmy backed into the pet food display by the door. Cans and bags and boxes of pet food fell every which way. Just as Jimmy looked over at his wife to come help him, and the manager looked like he was ready to throw Jimmy out, in walked Jimmy's mama and Jimmy's grandmamma.

When Jimmy told them what happened, Jimmy's mama stuck her chin in the air and the little brown mole on her cheek started to quiver. She told the manager it was all his fault; he should not have put the pet food so close to the door. Jimmy's grandmamma patted Jimmy, who was bent over with an armful of *Feline Felicity,* and said for him not to worry, the manager would pick it all up. The manager, who first engaged in a short staring contest with Jimmy's grandmamma, did. Surely he reckoned that these were good customers, good customers who would run their gums around the whole town if anything went against their way. Jimmy's grandmamma and Jimmy's mama and Jimmy all watched the manager clean up the mess, while Jimmy's wife kept on packing grocery sacks.

Afterwards, Jimmy's mama put her arm around Jimmy, and Jimmy's grandmamma held the door open for him. They went out of the store to the parking lot without so much as saying one word to Jimmy's wife, though they did say goodbye to the manager, who shook Jimmy's hand so Jimmy's mama and grandmamma could see he wasn't upset.

Jimmy's wife finished up the sacks she was packing, put them into a grocery cart for her customer, and rolled out just in time to see Jimmy's grandmamma crank up her car. When the car started to roll, there came an awful screech from under the fender, like a cat in a heat-fight somewhere.

Jimmy's mama and Jimmy's grandmamma got out of the car and looked up over the right front wheel, and turned pale as a moon. Jimmy didn't move from the front seat, but Jimmy's wife thought that even through the filthy window glass she saw tears in his eyes. She took two packages of meat out of a plastic bag in her cart and gave the bag to Jimmy's mama. She didn't hang around to see how they scraped Jimmy's Cat off the wheel. She rolled her cart back into the store.

At five o'clock, Jimmy's wife left her job and, instead of turning right, as she'd done every day before then, she turned left and then drove out of town on Highway 52. Before she got to the Interstate, she stopped to buy a tabloid magazine at what she remembered as an old,

175

family-owned grocery store. Now, hanging up and down the parking lot and all through the newly-painted building, were lots of red and yellow flags, along with signs that read, "Under New Management." When she went to pay for her magazine, she noticed that the clerk, a girl about her own age, was looking at her like she was trying to remember something. Then the clerk slapped the tabloid magazine down so hard on the counter that Jimmy's wife jumped. One last time.

"Hey, I know you!" the girl said. "Aren't you—?"

Jimmy's wife was just about to say yes, she was Jimmy's wife when the girl gave a loud "Uh huh!" then snapped her fingers and said, "You're Della Duval, the smartest girl in sixth-period Civics, remember?"

So tonight, in The New Life Motel, one hundred miles from Rangertown, I, Della Duval, the smartest girl in sixth-period Civics, am propped up in bed, reading a tabloid magazine, with my glasses on. And I don't believe I'll miss Jimmy's Cat one little bit, though I did try to love it.

Moon Dance: A Love Story

Every night, when she makes her rounds, she finds us watching the Georgia moon. We lie together in a single bed to catch the first inkling of its light and nightly mark its swell from miniscule to magnificent. We tell her of its essence, that it is something much bigger and brighter than itself. She gives us a condescending, "Uh huh, Shugah;" then leans over to tuck the white sheet around our thighs, and brush a dark hand across our foreheads. She smells of honey.

In the darkness, we point out to her the way the moon takes center stage to a sparkle of dancing stars, how it soon becomes distorted, fades and passes, leaving only a promise of return. We tell her that return is certain—our covenant between nothing and everything, between life and death. But she only wrinkles her sweet, black face and smiles, a tall silhouette against the silver light from the window.

"Night night, Miz Anna," she says.

I expect her to give us a kiss goodnight, but instead she gives us a pill for pain. On her way out, she does not close the window. She does not shut our door. We do not allow her to do that, because we will not be fastened here forever.

The artificial light from the hall draws a triangular shape on the linoleum, pierces the soft splash of moonlight that spreads downward from the foot of our bed. The illumination of the hall is soon extinguished by a human hand, but we lie in a radiance the human hand does not control. In the night, we speak of the covenant, the promise in death. I see its purpose. Death is passage. Death is close.

One hundred and six years old, both of us, we've held many who passed before us, held them in our arms as they took a last breath—parents, children, grandchildren, others we loved. I tell Will that God's desires are greater than our own. He accepts the truth in that. Then we speak of our daughter, our first child.

We were sixteen when she was born, and we named her Annalee; Anna after my own name, and Lee, the maiden name of Will's mother. We lost three other children after Annalee came to us: a girl, too small to be born, another from consumption when she was a month old, and a son, killed by the fever before he was two. But Annalee was different; we blamed cruelty for taking her, human malice with no face or name. And we cried, "Who would do this?"

When you are old, there are painful things to be remembered. In the moonlight, your page, your time on earth—all this will be read to you, all in one moment. Listen. In silence you will hear the story of your life, the whisperings of God leading you through it.

Annalee was a small-boned girl of five when she died. I used to watch her play with the dolls I made from corn cobs wrapped with cotton. I made clothes for the dolls, too. With my passed-down needle and thimble and thread, I sewed smiles into their faces like my own mama had done for me, sweet-bowed smiles like Annalee's.

There were three dolls: a mama, a daddy, and a baby doll. She'd named them after the three of us—Will, Anna, and Little Annalee. Will grinned at that. He liked it that his child thought so much of him. Having something named after him made him feel like a man when he was no more than a boy.

Annalee cared for those dolls as if each one had real life within it. At night, she made a place for them in her bed, the baby between the mother and father. Then she sang them to sleep. In the daytime, she carried all three wherever she went. She had them with her in the pocket of her pinafore when she died. Thank God she had them with her.

The woods beyond our house were beautiful in the fall, bronze and gold from the oaks and viridian green from the pines. Their deep purple shadows spread over a carpet of brown straw; all lovely, but Annalee and I liked the tall Pyracanthea tree best—its fiery red berries on glossy leaves, like nature's decorated Christmas tree. The berries were poisonous, of course, and the tree couldn't be climbed on account of its thorns. Yet beneath its overhanging bough lay a perfect little room for playing house, for making up stories, laughing, singing, for looking out, and feeling safe inside. It was not a place for a child to die, yet that cruelty came. After she had experienced death and destruction, my grandmother, Mama Fiddie, once told me, "God does not will cruelty. Always there comes justification." I have never forgotten her words, or the bitter tone that came with them.

When Will and I married in 1917, his daddy gave us eighty acres of good farmland alongside Black Snake Creek, on the Georgia side of the Chattahoochee River. His daddy and his two brothers helped us build our house out of heart pine. It had a front porch and four rooms with a kitchen out back and an outhouse beyond that. Mama Fiddie sewed curtains and made mattresses for our beds. She had Old Chollie bring her from Cuthbert, forty miles in the wagon, and they stayed most of two weeks; Old Chollie chopping piles of wood for the winter, and Mama Fiddie sewing and sewing. I missed them a good deal after they left.

Mama Fiddie was my mama's mother. Phalba was her given name, but when they were children, Old Chollie called her Miz Fiddie, so the name stuck. She took me as hers when my own mama died of yellow fever. Mama Fiddie was a Story before she married a Hornsby. She's the one who picked Will for me to marry; worked it out with Will's daddy, her second cousin once removed.

Families stayed close then, moved from place to place together. The Storys and the Hornsbys came together from South Carolina to South Georgia. And cousins often married cousins. But, in spite of all these arrangements beyond our control, I must have been agreeable to Will; he's never seemed dissatisfied in any deep way. As for myself, I couldn't have found a better man on my own; long-legged and tall, over six feet, with black curly hair and skin that never ceased to flush pink at the sight of a girl undressing in front of him.

Sometimes I did that, just to see him flush. Then I'd giggle, and hug him, and push him down on the bed Mama Fiddie made for us, all soft with straw and peanut shells and such. And when the moonlight came through the window, silvering our skin, we rose together, and danced. Oh, the joy God gave us in the warmth of each other's arms.

When Annalee was born, Will refused to be sent to the porch. He was there, right beside Aunt Sarah, Old Chollie's wife, so he could hear our baby's first cry. Mama Fiddie sent Aunt Sarah a month before the birth because she herself had come down with the cough and didn't want to spread it. Aunt Sarah rode a mule those forty miles from Cuthbert, just to be with me. It was her sweet black face that Annalee saw when she opened her little eyes to the world. "Thank you, Sweet Jesus," Aunt Sarah said, "for another child a' God." Oh, did Will smile then!

We had kind neighbors all around us, except down creek where the Samsons lived. Mr. Samson was a farmer, too, but Will said it was just a cover for bootlegging. There was no Mrs. Samson, only two colored men that helped Mr. Samson out, and his own three boys. One of his sons, the youngest, wasn't right, but all of them were mean as snakes. Usually, we only saw them at church meetings, where the youngest son took pleasure in taunting Annalee, snatching her dolls and grinding them in the dirt beneath his boot while she cried. Mr. Samson did nothing to stop him, so there was more than one fistfight between Will and Mr. Samson's mindless son.

The War Between the States was still fresh then. We were only a generation past being a conquered country after all. Mama Fiddie lived through the defeat. She sent her husband and five sons to the war. Three of her sons were killed, one lost a leg, and one had his palate shot out so that he never spoke again. Only her husband escaped without a wound. He came back to work their land. But Mama Fiddie's husband had been a Confederate officer during the War. Afterwards, when he refused to take the Oath of Allegiance to the Union, the government punished him by taking all he had: three hundred acres on Broad River in South Carolina, land their families had settled in 1755, and fought for in the Revolution; after that he was put in prison, where he died alone.

When the Storys and Hornsbys left for southwest Georgia, Mama Fiddie went with them. She packed up her two wounded sons, her two little girls, and the few belongings she had left: some tattered cloth, her needles, and a sterling silver thimble that her husband had once given her. She hid the thimble from Union soldiers by sewing it into her petticoat; it meant that much to her.

They left behind stolen farmland, left behind their homes, their schools, left it all; their churches now burned to the ground, their livestock slaughtered. They passed similar misfortunes all the way to the Chattahoochee. Oh, is it any wonder that thorns of meanness and resentment pricked into their hearts, or that Mama Fiddie daily sewed sorrow into her salvaged cloth, a tapestry, knotted and tied with pictures of her beloved dead?

Even now that bitterness fills me, until Will touches my shoulder, curls his body around mine, and says, "It's more a wonder that kindness can still be found in those same anguished hearts."

His heart is good. He has forgiven the transgressions of others against him. Yet he will not trust that he, himself, can be forgiven. For Will once killed an innocent man.

I kiss the nape of his neck, remembering when he wasn't here beside me, but alone in the room across the hall, still miserable in the shadow of his sin. Then one evening he simply appeared in my doorway, taut and dark-haired and smiling, as on those first Sunday nights of our marriage, when I tugged him from our bed to dance with me in the moonlight. A boy in love with the girl who loved him.

Beyond his shoulder, I see Mama Fiddie's sterling silver thimble. It sits where I have put it, between the window pane and its wooden sill, to keep from locking out hope. For years, I have taken the thimble from the cloth I wrapped it in—the tapestry sewn with pictures of those gone before us—and placed it there. In the light of each rising moon, it appears like a tiny beacon, pointing to a place where the weight of time is taken away. When the moon is full, I lift the window high above the tool that helped embroider our pasts, and say to Will, "Come. Dance with me in the moonlight."

He refuses. Always, He refuses.

Morning, we position ourselves just so we can see into the hall, but no one *out there* can gawk at us. Let them come inside if they want to see that we're still breathing. We watch the sun spread across the grass, browned from the drought of this Georgia summer. Will says there'll be no harvest for those who farm; no peanuts, no cotton, no keep for their families. There *will* be suffering.

At times, it was the same for us. We waited for water. We grieved for our lost children. We suffered. We prayed. And we did not die. In the end, our crops were given rain, and we were given one more child, who lived long enough to have a son himself.

She comes again, a smile on her sweet, black face, to bring our breakfast, to give more pills. She is kind, but we will not get attached to her. The nice ones never stay long.

"Your grandson's here," she says, helping me from the bed to the rocking chair--Mama Fiddie's chair, cane-backed, with curved wooden arms, and brown leather seat. She sets breakfast on a tray, puts a napkin in my lap. "I'll check back in a few minutes," she says as she leaves.

Will and I hear James's familiar footsteps, quick and purposeful. Our grandson has set a mission for himself. He is writing our history because he wants to know his own. His long, thin shape is framed between the wall of our room and the door's edge. "Good morning, Mamaw," he says. His hair has become white. How can this be?

Our grandson is a lawyer who defends the guilty. In frank moments, when he isn't afraid of coming across as vain, he calls himself an advocate of mercy. James kisses my face, but does not kiss Will, though his grandfather leans toward him. Our grandson reaches into a bulky bag and pulls out a tape recorder. Pressing a red button, he sets it beside the rocking chair, on the waxed linoleum. He has Will's almond eyes and his smile is sweet, same as when Will held him and sang to him in the old cane rocker, like a fragile glass treasure in his arms, a baby with no father and a mother gone crazy over the news of her husband's death.

The telegram came just as the war was over, the day the boy was born. *"We regret to inform you that . . . "* His father, the only child left to us, killed in the islands of the Pacific. His mother took her love letters, her two older girls, and disappeared forever. But she didn't take her infant boy. Him she left with us. We fed him, clothed him, read to him, taught him to read and to love. We gave him all we knew of the chapter titles of life. Now, he wants to fill in the words. But I want something more from him. Something greater.

I smell his cologne as he leans forward to pull his bulky bag closer. "You've been so good about telling the

185

stories, Mamaw. Now, will you tell me about Annalee's murder?" He asks this so suddenly, I take in a breath. I expect some compassion, but his eyes are emotionless as a tree toad's as he continues, "After all these years, I mean to solve it, once and for all. I'd like you to tell me what you remember." He *is* a determined lawyer, after all.

"Let your grandfather tell it." I look at Will.

Our grandson seems startled, as if I've shouted, when my words were only a whisper, only as loud as I could make them. His eyes have widened, warm and kindhearted now. "Oh, Mamaw," he says, gently, and puts his hands around mine, lifting them from my lap as one might lift a tiny, injured bird, fallen from a tree. I used to take his hands in the same way when he was a school boy, when he was nodding into sleep, weary of his home lessons. "Pay attention," I used to say gently. I expect him to say the same to me, but that is not what he says.

"Don't you remember? Granddaddy Will is dead. He died ten years ago, in the room across the hall."

He most certainly did not! He's right here, beside me.

If you were a boy again, I'd swat your bottom for that lying nonsense.

As if he hasn't heard me, he reaches for his bag and says, "If you're not well, I'll come back another time."

No, don't leave. I turn to Will again, and see him hesitate. My throat as dry as the summer drought, but with effort, I try to make myself heard. "Your grandfather will tell you what you want to know."

My husband rises slowly from the bed and sits in the vinyl chair by the window, his muscular thighs pressed against the firmness, a strand of hair, shiny as a blackbird's wing, tumbling onto his smooth forehead. He gives me a look of pain that is a plea. *Help,* it says.

Our grandson's eyes follow me as I rise, too, to sit next to Will in his cold vinyl chair. His body warms mine, as it has for the ninety years of our marriage. I've never regretted those years. Even when he failed, I forgave him. Forgiveness is required after a promise to love. At least, it used to be so.

Our grandson's expression is one of doubt, but he presses another button on the tape recorder. I notice the small dimple on his chin, exactly like Will's. "Tell me what you remember about Annalee's death." I know he will not stay unless we do.

Will tenses beside me. He appears overcome, as if I must speak for him. And so, I try to.

I thought he would never get over it, the morning we found her little body beneath the pyracantha. Will held her to his heart, gave one long moan; then his sorrow turned to rage. His child was dead. Dead. Immediately he was sure it was the youngest Samson boy, the one stupid from birth, who had strangled Annalee. "Out of meanness," he said to me. "He done it out of meanness." As sure as Cain killed Abel. And none of my protests could change what he meant to do. So, Will lynched him; an innocent man, but my husband didn't know it when he strung him up.

Our grandson acts as if he's heard nothing, as if he's waiting for me to begin. "I was once told that Grandfather hung an innocent man," he says, fiddling with the tape recorder. He waits for my response. I give him an affirmative nod.

And then our grandson, James, a lawyer who spends his life arguing for reprieve, shakes his head reproachfully. A reaction I did not expect. As if such a thing has never before happened on earth. As if innocent Jesus Himself hadn't been the victim of angry men, hadn't, in spite of this, begged His Father to forgive the murderers. I am disappointed at the dearth of compassion from my own kin.

Will looks down, puts a hand against his forehead. I'm certain he is remembering the man's last pitiful gasp for life as he swung from the limb of a tree. When I reached him that night he was on his knees beneath the tree, crying inconsolably. Two deaths, already, in that one day; I worried there would be three.

But our grandson is studying me with grave eyes, as if he's wondering if I will ever answer his questions.

We had a beautiful funeral for Annalee. Nice funerals for all our children, but for Annalee we tried to make it special, so maybe, if even looking on from afar, those who did such things could see that there is more goodness than meanness in the world. I might not know the answers to so many problems that wreck this world. But let me tell you one thing. God is in the span of time between darkness and light. Little by little, like the moon, He shows His reflection, and patiently waits for us to ask Him into the dance.

Then my own tears come. I can't hold them back. Our grandson comes toward me, puts an arm around my shoulders. "We don't have to talk today, Mamaw."

Oh, but I do. At first, Will believed without qualms that what he'd done was right, but in the days that followed, we learned the truth. Despite its thorns, Annalee had climbed the tree all by herself, had slipped beyond our watch and care, and had broken her neck when she fell from it. It was then I saw enough torment in Will's face to last a lifetime, enough that he confessed his violence, enough that he asked pardon of the bootlegger, Samson, for the lynching of his son. Mr. Samson gave no pardon. The jury showed a little compassion, though. Still, Will spent five years in prison.

Our grandson's face is strained, and I can see that he *feels* my tears, but he strokes my arm as if I've said nothing. "Besides your husband, you lost your children, all except my Dad," he murmurs, as if he's talking to himself.

Why won't you listen? I accepted Annalee's death long ago, and the deaths of my other children, too! (Have I just snapped at him?) I *know* they are with God. It's your grandfather I'm worried about. He paid a penalty on earth for what he did, and begged God's mercy. Yet now he despairs that God would love him enough to forgive him.

"Separation from those we love is hard," our grandson says. His expression is potent with pity.

I try to shout *Pity your grandfather! Be* God's *advocate! Tell him God is waiting to offer him a more wondrous place than this.*

But no words come from my mouth.

Our grandson says, "You're too weak to talk now, Mamaw. I'll come again when you're stronger."

Though I love him, he's not the advocate I've waited for.

I don't want him to leave. I want him to live up to his vocation. But he kisses me, and he is gone.

All seems just as it was before our grandson came. Inside, the air remains cool, and the artificial plants have no thirst in a world afraid of discomfort.

Except it is not as it was. Will turns his boyish eyes to the opened, paned window. Beyond it, the sun infuses our guarded ground with an eclipse of cross-shaped shadows that cool the parched earth. The cones of a long-leafed pine, like a crown of thorns, have fallen into a bed of zinnias and daisies, their stems bent in authentic thirst. Azaleas without blooms, their leaves the color of a faded dollar bill, still champion the walkway.

I say to my husband, "See? We are surrounded by an offer of mercy. Take hold of it. It's waiting for both of us."

A hungry raven pecks the pavement, finding only pebbles, until another, one with a red berry in its beak, comes to compensate. Will watches the two fly off together, then turns to me. I see a small change.

I remind him of another summer without water, the drought from which God saved us. I remind him that after we had suffered through it all, new life grew within me. I tell him, finally, to expect the same. Then I touch his shoulder.

He ponders my words.

The moon is rising now. Again, she comes to make her rounds. By the end of the week, she tells us, she will leave here for good. She has decided to accept a more-than-generous offer in another place.

"God is good, Miss Anna!" she says, kissing my cheek, completing her nightly duties with joy, leaving with a smile.

I am sorry to see her go, but my heart is happy, too. Will has heard the good news. His face glimmers as he takes my hand and says that it's time for us to leave here, too. We follow the silver ribbon of light to the window, and, at long last, see the way out from this world. The light traces the turn of Will's face, caresses the slope of his shoulders, and a boy of sixteen embraces forgiveness, and then the girl who has loved him for as long as she has lived.

Come, Will, I say. Dance with me in the moonlight.

This time, he doesn't refuse.

The Pleasure of Company: A Ghost Story

A year ago, when she could not bear to speak to a soul, when she did not comb her hair or wash her face or dab herself with lavender water, or wear her corset (because any underclothing cut off her breath), Julia began the night walks into the woods, taking off her gown and lying upon the ground beneath the ancient oak. But neither the cooling breeze upon her breasts nor the sparkle of stars kissing the leaves to silver against the dark sky lifted her melancholy. The night walks have become her futile attempt to make sense of meanness. Still Julia cannot fathom a reason for the death of her child; still she has no face for Hattie's murderer.

Clara and I come.

We follow her home. The next morning, Clara and I watch as Joseph, Julia's husband, instructs Esther to, "Restart the clocks, uncover the mirrors, and draw open the curtains in Miss Julia's bedroom."

Julia protests. "Joseph, it's too soon."

"It's been a year, exactly," Joseph says, motioning Esther to begin. He is a tall, thin man, with a once-pleasant face, now pinched by sorrow and the worry of a much older man.

The old black woman, Julia's childhood nurse, carefully lifts the customary black satin from the mirror on the dressing table. The light causes Julia to shut her eyes and lower her chin into the high-necked collar of her funeral dress, made from the same bolt of satin that covered the windows and mirrors. Every night, Esther washes and irons it for Julia because she'll wear nothing else.

"What if Hattie's spirit has been trapped behind the mirror?" Julia asks.

"The covering of mirrors is just superstition," Joseph says. "Hattie has not been trapped. She has not been kept from Heaven."

Clara and I hear and understand his thinking; that the only trapped spirit is Julia's, and he desperately wants to help it escape.

He motions Esther out of the room so he can be alone with his wife. In the uncovered glass, her unkempt brown hair hangs about her oval-shaped face. Her narrow shoulders slump forward and her opaque eyes, once buoyantly blue with the promise of a happy life, are as tarnished as neglected silver. He has to do something meaningful soon, before he loses her forever.

Yesterday, he suggested a dinner party. Once, she loved celebrations. "The dinner party is what you need, Julia," he reminds her. "You've not had the pleasure of company for more than a year." He bends to kiss her cheek, but she shies away from him as she has come to do, giving a bitter wince at the touch of his fingers on the nape of her neck.

"A dinner party will not give me pleasure," she says. "It's for you, your politics."

Joseph has become a familiar figure on the streets of Tuscaloosa as the new county Tax Assessor. Yes he has a

194

reputation to keep, but all he wants now is to keep his wife from crying. He knows she loves him, whatever love means. "I loved you the first moment I saw you, and I will never stop loving you, Joseph Shelley." Those words she used to say.

"The party will not be for my politics," he insists, his voice splintering. "It's only for you."

Standing behind her in the mirror, Joseph longs to touch his wife, to hold her in his arms again. Longs to explain how sorry he is that the old terrors came upon him that day . . . came and took him out of his mind. But he can't go that deeply into his own soul. He can't ask for her forgiveness without admitting what he did to her, and to their daughter. Hattie is dead. *Joseph* is the reason. Julia doesn't know this. She'd never suspect this. No one would.

She turns to him then, and sees grief carved around his eyes.

And he sees the sense of duty, still in hers.

She puts a hand on his arm. "Alright," she says, feeling the risk tingling in her throat. "I'll try."

Mr. and Mrs. Joseph Shelley

Request the Pleasure of Your Company

For Dinner at Eight

In their Home

2703 Seventh Street

Tuscaloosa, Alabama

Saturday, July 28, 1880

R.S.V.P

Julia forces herself to write and address the notes of invitation, and Joseph has them delivered by a special messenger. For the next two weeks she worries over the dinner. Brief moments come when she feels she can resume life as it had been and serve as mistress of her house, and as her husband's hostess. Other moments come too, she does not know why they come, when she mistrusts everyone, even Joseph.

She's ashamed to have such misgivings. In the aftermath of Hattie's death, Joseph seemed as devastated as she was. He saw to it that Hattie's body was laid out in the corner of the parlor and watched over every moment until they gave her proper burial, by Esther, or himself, or their younger son, Samuel, who stood straight and unblinking beside the box that held his sister, occasionally poking her cheek with his boyish finger to be sure she was dead.

Esther washed the child's body and dressed Hattie in a pink silk dress with a high lace collar to cover the bruising around her neck, then Joseph laid her within the white satin lining of the coffin. For nearly a week, Hattie remained there for the many acquaintances coming to offer their condolences, with her slender arms around the porcelain doll Joseph had given her on her seventh birthday. During that time, Julia entered the parlor only once. She went in alone, and though she was not yet thirty, she came out as one who has passed into a world far from the present moment.

Julia did not attend the interment. No one could remove her gripping hands from the arms of the rocking chair in Hattie's bedroom, or rouse her from the glassy-eyed state in which she remained with that one, continuous thought clasping her mind: who would kill her child?

It was Stella, their youngest daughter, who found a way into Julia's soul again. Night after night, she climbed into her mother's lap, and night after night took her mother's hands in her hands and wrapped her mother's arms around her own lonely body, until a time came when Julia noticed her baby, and remembered that she loved Stella, too.

On Saturday, the day of the dinner party, Julia sits before the canted glass mirror of her dressing table. She's gotten no further in dressing than her pantaloons and camisole, picturing speculations in the eyes of her soon arriving guests, and imagining that, seeing her, they would question one another behind white-gloved hands, "Poor Julia. Will she ever be herself again?" A question for which Julia has no answer.

As the late afternoon sun angles across the floor, the mellow gold frame, with its pierced shell cresting and floral tendrils, encircles her image. Julia leans forward to study her reflection in the glass. Her face shows the constant rake inside her, a terrible battle between trust and fear, between what is apparent, and what it is not. Her image is not as she remembers it. She is not who she used to be.

Upon the dressing table is the lachrymatory into which she daily sheds her tears. It is closed with a stopper, so that nothing evaporates from the tiny, crystal vial. After the uncovering of the mirrors, she hid the lachrymatory from Esther who wanted to take it away. Next to the vial is a larger bottle—Joseph's promise of relief.

Some months ago, he gave her the absinthe to dull her pain and help her forget what happened, and, perhaps, because he himself was tired of her unhappiness, had been made miserable by her unhappiness. A mere sip of absinthe produces velvet numbness. Again, she takes it, without the usual spoonful of sugar, without water. She swallows its emerald bitterness, dabs the residual from her lips with a lace handkerchief, and feels the usual caged fluttering beneath her breast. She watches the muscles relax in her face. Still, the mirror does not show her as she used to be.

"Julia?" she whispers, and reaches to touch her image. Her fingers against the glass seem foreign, seem to push her back into solitude. But Julia is not alone. She is not without company. We are here, and it is time.

Clara and I await her recognition. Ghosts from the past. Grandparents who love her.

She doesn't see our reflection until Clara reaches around her slim shoulders and lifts a hairbrush from the dressing table. Then every rise of bone, every shadow of skin, becomes clear in the timeless mirror. Past, Present and Future are one.

"Grandfather? Grandmother?" She doesn't appear surprised. Julia was always receptive to things out of the ordinary. And, to be sure, this is no ordinary moment.

Clara and I never knew a happier child, or one who loved us more. She smiles for the first time in a long while, then her eyes deepen, and we know immediately that she will ask about Hattie. "Your child is contented," Clara says quickly.

"But Grandmother, who would kill my child?"

Our hearts ache for her, but it is not up to us to reveal the answer.

"Give her the gift, Francis," Clara says to me.

I take the doll from inside my waistcoat, the doll Joseph laid in Hattie's coffin, and lay it upon the dressing table. Its porcelain lips are still pink, and its fragile fingers are open, as in a caress.

We allow time for more of her tears, comforting her as best we can. We remind her of the presence of love in which Hattie resides. Julia admits to that, but still she questions, "Who took her life?"

I reach to stroke her hair as I used to.

"No, Francis," Clara says. "She barely has time to dress for the party. Julia has company to prepare for."

Clara sets the brush to Julia's hair, sweeping it away from her face and wrapping the length around her head. "You must always look your prettiest," Clara reminds her, arranging Julia's hair into a crest of ash-brown curls as she used to do when Julia lived with us in our South Carolina home.

"Now, stand," Clara orders, and Julia rises while Clara fits the long stays around her middle and laces them up and down until Julia's waist is pulled to nearly nothing. Oh, she's so thin now!

Clara drops the crinoline petticoat into a ring on the floor and Julia steps into it. Clara draws it up and ties it, then takes an apple-green silk taffeta from its hanger and slips it over Julia's head.

"I ought to be in black, and buttoned up," Julia says. "The neckline is much too low for bereavement, and the sleeves are too high a puff."

"Nonsense, you are beautiful," Clara says. "Beauty is power to a woman, and necessary for control of her house. I think we need a bit more attention to your hair." Together, they pat and poke and stroke down any stray strands. Finally, Clara surveys Julia's image in the mirror. "You are exquisite, darling." Her words are not an empty compliment.

"I'm not sure my heart is ready, Grandmother."

"There'll be no tears tonight," Clara says gently. "It's time for the mourning to end." And into Julia's curls, she sticks a jade and pearl jeweled comb. "A gift from your grandfather. It belonged to his mother."

"I remember," Julia says, her eyes catching mine. "Look, Grandfather. I still have this." She opens the drawer of her dressing table and takes another piece of my mother's jewelry, an intricately carved cameo I gave to her when her own mother was dying, one of many Prussian treasures crowded into a trunk for my boyhood passage to America. I am touched by the care with which she attaches it to the bodice of her gown.

"Stand up straight," Clara says. "Don't slump." An instruction she often gave the girl we raised.

Julia rises from her chair and stands before us, absolutely regal. Clara is pleased, and I am pleased, too. In the twist of a single night, we will see Julia come back to herself. Once more, she will preside as mistress of the house on Seventh Street, and preserve her husband's adoration of her.

Clara hurries to help Julia into a pair of long white gloves, then hands her an ivory fan painted with flowers. "We're ready to go down now," Clara says.

Julia doesn't budge. Her eyes are set on the emerald bottle.

"Alright, just a bit more," Clara sighs and offers her the absinthe. "Be careful not to spill any of it on your dress, darling." And we follow Julia downstairs.

The dining room table is ready. Placed upon it is the old china, hand-painted with wide-winged birds of prey, and so finely fired that when a plate is held before the tangerine light of candles, the hand behind it is clearly seen.

The fragile china once belonged to Clara, passed down by her own grandmother. Clara used to inspect each piece, taking note of the flaws of time--chips, cracks, any sign of unfavorable wear. As was her trait, she repaired it, and then returned it to its proper place behind the glass doors of the mahogany cabinet. Reparation is still what Clara does best.

On the table, between the candelabras, sits a large bowl of deep, blue-green ferns interspersed with four kinds of flowers of particular meaning: white myrtles for love and marriage, bronze zinnias for thoughts of absent loved ones, rhododendron for risk, and thistle and goldenrod for defiance and precaution.

It was Joseph who chose the myrtles. A few days ago, he drove the wagon thirty miles back to the old home place in Greene County to get them because they'd been Julia's favorite. He cut the blooms from three flowering trees he'd planted just after Hattie's birth, when he and Julia lived there.

The bronze zinnias were decided upon by Samuel and Stella, in memory of their older sister, and as comfort to their mother. Last Spring, with Esther's help, they planted the seeds in the side garden of the new house on Seventh Street, within view of Julia's bedroom. In the evening light, she watched her children's fingers turn the earth, but the following Fall, after Hattie's death, when the mass of copper colors prompted by their hands came forth, she barely noticed the miracle.

Esther insisted on rhododendrons from the yard, packed around the front porch like soldiers guarding the house. The flowers rise wild, require no real care, and yet become beautiful without it. Julia considered their pink rowdiness and called it "a flouting against proper taste," but for the dinner party, she deferred to Esther.

The thistle and goldenrod were of Julia's own choosing. Clara set the thought of them in our granddaughter's mind. She'd known it would be an effort for Julia to retrieve them; the stalks of goldenrod were at the edge of the woods, but the thistles grew within the shadows of the tight, tall pines surrounding the place where Hattie had died. Yet, Julia took courage and gathered them.

"You're still the strong mistress of your house," Clara says now. It's necessary to re-establish that."

Joseph is at the bottom of the staircase as Julia comes down. He turns, surprised to see his wife looking as she used to. He opens his hand to the air as she descends, as if to grab her before she slips away again.

When she reaches him, he kisses her. He speaks gently, for he has become a milder man, a repentant man. "I'll watch out for you, Julia." Though she's uncertain about that, she takes his arm.

We enter the dining room. It is Julia's room of service, where bread is perpetually broken and placed into hands that sometimes hold joy, other times enough misfortune to strangle a happy heart.

We pass the table and its chairs, caned in decades-old memories and still pungent with the breath of earth. Clara is pleased to see our ornate side-board displayed with some fare of the food that will come. There are crabs and oysters, secured by a friend of Joseph's, whose steamboat ships cotton to Mobile. There are apples and walnuts brought by Joseph himself from the old fruit orchard in Greene County. The fruit is arranged in large sterling compotes embellished with silver grapes. The rest of the food will be served when it is time: beef and venison, chicken and wild duck accompanied by beetroot, cabbage and potatoes, pears and stuffed dates.

Beneath the china, silver shapes of shadows dance upon the white damask cloth, from two towering candelabras on a table set for ten. Cut—glass crystal goblets are burnished by the candlelight with brilliant images that skip across cups and plates. The light invokes memory, and origin. Always, it is essential to know what came before.

•

All in this room was once ours, Clara's and mine. It's here today only because we buried it in the tilled, spring earth of the cornfield beside our South Carolina home— weeks ahead of the Federal troops. Julia's father, our son William, sent word to us from his Confederate camp in Virginia that General Sherman's men were coming.

At once, we sent Julia and her sickly mother to the home of her relatives in Alabama. I pled with Clara to go with them, but she was always a stubborn woman, and wouldn't leave me. Then Clara and I began to dig. We dug for weeks, aided by Esther, only a child at the time, and her older brother, George. We hollowed out a tremendous hole, the depth and width of twenty graves, in which to lay our possessions, and keep them from thievery.

The first thing we lowered into it was the mahogany dining table, with its tapered scrolling legs pointing upward. In its belly we placed the rest; the oak china cabinet, the cherry sideboard, the chairs with deeply scalloped crest rails and curved stiles. We wrapped the china, crystal, and jewelry in damask linens, and covered it all with the earth that fed us.

Then we planted corn. By the time the Yankees arrived, the green tips of our trickery were beginning to show, but there was no sign of value for them to steal. So, they stole our livestock—every cow, every chicken we owned. Then they set fire to the barn, and headed for the house with their torches. When I tried to stop them, they halted me with a bullet instead. They halted Clara, too, when she rushed to my side.

She knelt beside me and whispered, "We'll go to heaven hand in hand." And we surely did, though we were fifty years old then, and too young to die.

George ran away, while Esther hid in a fox's hole, living on berries and pine seeds for months. She was still hiding when our son, William, finally came home from the War and found her. He took her with him, away from South Carolina, to Greene County, Alabama, to be with his ailing wife, and his daughter, Julia.

William became postmaster of the little community of Boligee, and there, Julia's mother succumbed to the last of many illnesses, dying of yellow fever. The fever took our son, William, too. So, our South Carolina land and treasures rightfully came to Julia. She was a child then, and had no means to retrieve them, so the land stayed vacant, and our treasures remained beneath the cornfield, buried for years.

As for Joseph, he was thirteen when he ran away from Boligee, where he was born, to join the Alabama Cavalry. He was quickly captured in the woods of North Georgia, and taken to a Federal prison camp in Ohio. God only knows how he survived those eight months before the War was over, except that Joseph was a good man who turned his mind to others.

In the camp was his commanding officer, Colonel Isaac Jameson, who had been wounded, and, because of his rank, was singled out for starvation. Joseph stole bits of food and water from the Yankee tents to save his life —until he was caught and thrown into a dark, wood-covered hole for months. It was rumored a Yankee sergeant out for revenge made Joseph his personal whipping boy because an Alabama Confederate from Greene County had shot and killed his older brother. The sergeant beat him day and night until Joseph's ribs were broken, and his back bleeding and rotting from infection. The vengeful sergeant even tried to poison him with belladonna, extracted from the deadly Night Shade bush, the cause of his hallucinations.

When Joseph returned home he was no more than a bent skeleton, and most believed he was quite mad. At first he wouldn't eat, fearing maggots, or poison, in any plate set before him. He wouldn't sleep, unless on his back, holding a simple kitchen knife across his chest. He washed himself in the river at least three times a day, believing his skin was rotting away . . . and frequently forgetting to redress afterward. He was often seen hunting naked in the woods, with no weapon except his bare hands. Everyone in Boligee expected he would fall to the wrath of a wild animal, but twice, he came home with a bear carcass slung about his bare shoulders.

If it hadn't been for his widowed, strong-armed mother, he'd eventually have come to harm. Her son's former commander, Confederate Colonel Isaac Jameson, made it known to her by letter that Joseph had saved him from certain death in the prison camp. For all that, Colonel Jameson wrote, he wanted to repay Joseph in any way he could.

His mother wrote back, and the Colonel came to Boligee to get Joseph. For nearly a year, he lived in Colonel Jameson's Tuscaloosa home, tended to by Colonel Jameson's personal doctor, and fed by the Colonel's mild-mannered wife, who soothed him most when she shared her emerald absinthe. When he finally came home to Boligee, he was docile as a lamb, with only a few occasional blackouts, so docile he had to be forced to do everything.

His mother compelled him to work in the post office with our son, William, who was still alive at the time. There, Joseph met Julia. He was just older enough in age to think her a child then, a wisp of a girl with her gaze constantly attached to him.

After William's death, Joseph's mother insisted the orphaned girl move into their house. Through a slight crack in her bedroom door, Joseph saw that Julia was no longer a little girl. The image of her bare back and slender thighs as she bent to the floor to pull the crinoline to her waist spurred passion in him, and he knew he would marry her.

After their wedding, Joseph seemed to forget the horrors he experienced in prison, except for a nightmare or two when the rain whipped against their bedroom window and beat upon the roof of their house. He would cry out in pain then, causing Julia no small concern over the terror in his dreams, though she never gave words to what she feared in secret.

Joseph worked at the post office for ten years, and, during that time, Hattie and Samuel were born. In those days, it was common for a father to favor his son. Joseph loved Samuel, but it was Hattie whom he adored. She was the image of Julia, with a laugh like the tinkling of a sterling spoon against crystal. "Let's play *Buried Treasure*, Daddy," she would say, hiding in some obvious place he'd pretend he didn't see, only to cry out, "Find me, Daddy. Find your buried treasure!"

He'd call out her name and search in and under all manner of things, until finally she would run giggling into his arms. "Here I am!"

Then Joseph received word that Colonel Jameson had nominated him for the position of Tax Assessor in Tuscaloosa. With Colonel Jameson's vigorous support, Joseph easily won the election, and moved Julia and their two children to Tuscaloosa, into the big house on Seventh Street where he and Julia were happy—for a time.

But soon Colonel Jameson died from the lingering results of scurvy he'd contracted in the Yankee prison camp, and Joseph's horrid nightmares returned. He thrashed violently in his sleep, as if shielding his body from an indescribable menace. Once, he awakened to find his fingers squeezing Julia's neck. So apologetic was he for the incident that as a recompense he hired two drivers with wagons to follow him to South Carolina, where he dug our treasures from the earth for Julia. Esther, who remembered the exact location, went with him. Julia insisted upon going, too. They brought it all back to their home in Tuscaloosa, where our treasured possessions took on a new beginning.

·

In the dining room, Esther tells Joseph that she's getting no assistance at all from those he employed to help her, especially not from Noah, the near-to-blind butler who can't see his hand in front of his face. "The people's gonna be here soon and I ain't finished dressing little Stella, and Samuel's already got a smudge of dirt on his new breeches."

Joseph is gazing at his beautiful wife. "I'll see to it," he says, without budging.

Clara spots a tiny, emerald droplet of absinthe on the corner of Julia's mouth, and wipes it away with a gloved hand.

Esther has her eyes on Julia, too. A strand of ash-brown hair loosens, slips over Julia's cheek, across the porcelain bone, rising high above the pinkness of her lips.

Esther goes to pin it back, and then whispers to Joseph, "Tonight's gonna be too much for Miss Julia. She don't look fit in the face. She's gonna leave us again. I just hope she don't go before they all come to eat dinner because somebody besides me got to give directions to the half-blind help."

Julia overhears. "Don't worry, Esther. I'm myself now."

The old woman gives a doubtful smile, but leaves to go finish with the children. Joseph ignores Esther's comment. He sees Julia as renewed, and is thankful for it.

"I am myself now," she repeats to Joseph.

She stands like a queen before him, the woman he's always loved. He regrets having thought of the dinner party, regrets the time he'll have to spend with their guests, and wants only to be with Julia, Julia as she used to be.

But already the invited guests are arriving. The gentlemen are in black waist-coats and jackets, the ladies are in formal evening dresses, and stately Julia greets each of them as if sorrow had never imposed its heavy tax upon her.

Esther brings in the children to be seen and admired by the guests. Samuel and Stella, like pristine angels, stand shyly before their mother. Julia drops to her knees beside them, kissing their cheeks, holding them to her breast. "I've missed you. I've missed you," she says.

Clara is quickly beside her, with a hand on Julia's waist lest she make a spectacle of herself in front of her guests. Julia rises, and takes charge again. "Beautiful children, and so well-behaved," is the consensus of her guests, who watch as Esther, her mouth drawn further downward, leads the children back upstairs.

Clara whispers a warning. "Remember your position in society, Julia, and the sober etiquette that goes with it."

Julia brushes Clara's cheek with a kiss. "I haven't forgotten, Grandmother. You can see I am myself now."

Let the guests be retained by the pleasant company, and cheered with the hope that, before the evening is over, there is something good still in store for them."
—*Hill's Manual of Social Forms, 1878*

Julia gathers us all into the drawing room with instilled decorum, instructing the gentlemen as to which lady they will escort to table. Finally, she turns to Joseph.

"Darling, will you escort Mrs. Jameson?" With a gloved hand Julia touches the shoulder of the deceased Colonel's elderly widow. Mrs. Jameson, who is hard of hearing, smiles as Joseph takes her arm for the dining room, and Joseph seems happy to have some normalcy again.

Entering the dining room is an elderly gentleman wearing the Confederate uniform of an officer, three stars on his collar. Clara has a coy smile on her face, but I know what she's done.

"It isn't your party, Clara! You shouldn't have invited Colonel Jameson."

"Of course I should have, he wanted to help with the repair. After all, Isaac Jameson has great affection for Joseph."

Julia is greeting him warmly. "Colonel Jameson, it is good to see you!" Very unusual, I'm thinking, since Julia doesn't seem a bit surprised at the presence of a dead man.

"If the Colonel is here for Joseph's repair," I ask Clara, "then why does Julia see him?"

My wife gives me a look of condescension. "He is *not* here for Joseph. He is here for Julia. People see who they need to see." Clara is definitely up to something.

"We are so grateful to you for coming, Colonel Jameson," Julia says. "Would you be kind enough to escort me to the table?"

Then Clara takes my arm, and the dinner party begins.

The place cards are positioned properly. The men and women are seated alternately down the table, with Mrs. Jameson to the right of Joseph, and Julia opposite her husband on the far end. Joseph observes that the chair to Julia's right is vacant, but the other seven guests, elite members of Tuscaloosa society, don't appear to notice. They are busy in polite conversation.

Joseph motions for Noah, the near-to-blind butler he hired for the evening. "Why is there is an extra place set at the table?"

The butler surveys the table, confused. "Sir," he whispers, "Where is the extra place?"

"To the right of my wife. Please remove it."

Noah squints and studies the table again. "But Mr. Joseph," he says, "Colonel Jameson's sitting next to Miss Julia. I don't think it'd be proper to take up his bowl while he's drinking the soup."

"Colonel Jameson?"

"Yes, sir."

"You see Colonel Jameson?"

"Yes sir, Mr. Joseph. He's talking to your wife."

"Isaac Jameson? Colonel Isaac Jameson?" His voice is too loud. The table is abruptly silent. He's been heard by everyone, except Mrs. Jameson who is concentrating on raising a soup spoon to her mouth without spilling its content.

Clara touches my hand. "See how delighted the Colonel is that Joseph has spoken his name?"

It's true. The old gentleman appears quiet flattered, and is waiting for Joseph to finish. Clara gives the Colonel a nod and an affectionate smile which he returns.

Julia turns a lifted chin to Joseph, along with the rest of their guests. Their host has called out Mr. Jameson's name, and they are waiting to hear what else he intends to say. Joseph is baffled, wondering how he should react.

"What do you mean to say, Joseph?" Julia asks.

He clears his throat. "I mean to say that—Isaac Jameson was a good man. Best man I knew. And tonight, his company is missed."

"Hear, hear," is the unified answer of the guests. All raise their glasses in a salute to one who has left the present world. All except Julia; Joseph's salute, along with the guests' response, puzzles her. She touches the quatrefoil on the Colonel's sleeve to be sure he is beside her.

Clara is gazing at the closed paneled doors leading into the parlor as if she expects someone else. Even in our new life, my wife is full of surprises.

"Alright, who is coming now?" I ask her.

Her eyes turn to Joseph. "Just look at him, Francis. He's barely able to live with what he's done. I had to do something special for him, didn't I?"

At once, the paneled doors fly open, as if pushed by a great wind. The guests' napkins flutter about. "Is there a storm coming?" one of them asks.

Joseph pushes away from the table and heads for the doors. Half-way there, he jolts backward as if he's run into an invisible wall. In the threshold stands his best-loved child, Hattie, dressed in a pink silk dress with a high, lace collar. The victim of his most tortuous nightmare is smiling up at him.

"Close the doors, Joseph," Julia urges. "Our guests are shuddering."

He edges around Hattie to latch the double doors, hoping that when he turns around, she'll be gone. He tells himself she's only in his imagination, another dreaded terror come upon him—one he deserves.

He never intended to strangle his own child, and has no memory of doing it. The terror came on him when he was playing with her in the woods, *Buried Treasure,* always her favorite game. "Find me Daddy!" was all he remembered, until she was dead in his arms and he heard his own wretched howl of horror.

In a daze, he'd carried her to the house, her body still warm, and limp as a newborn bird. Naturally, no one assumed he'd done it. They thought there was a murderer loose, an unknown murderer who'd killed Hattie, an *assassin* who could never hope to be redeemed. He hadn't known what to say to Julia. The sorrow in her face was unbearable, so he'd said nothing.

He slowly turns to see if Hattie is still there.

She is.

He is so frozen by fear that he cannot blink.

The guests, along with Julia, have gone back to their conversations. Noah is leading the servants in, with trays of beef and venison, chicken and wild duck. Surprisingly, the near-blind butler notices Hattie, too. He puts down his tray of food, ushers her to an ornate chair at the end of the sideboard, then approaches Joseph who's watching from the middle of the room.

"One of the children escaped from upstairs," Noah says. "Should I call Esther to come get her, or do you want her to stay here?"

"Let me stay, Daddy," Hattie says. Her voice is heard by no guest, but Joseph is too stunned to speak. Noah shrugs, and goes back to serving.

"I want to see Mama," Hattie says to her father.

Joseph turns away from her. She can't be real. Perspiring profusely, he struggles to get back to the table, praying that the tremors do not come, or the violent anger that accompanies them.

He's had only one such attack since Hattie's death, the first night Julia insisted on sleeping alone. That night, in the bedroom down the hall, where he's slept for the past year, the tremors came. The next morning the room was a shamble. There was blood on the wall, blood on his knuckles, and his forehead was cut just above his left eye. *If only I could rid myself of the terrors,* he is thinking now. *I'm,* he can barely say it. *I'm a danger to Julia—to everyone.*

The hum of the guests' banter rises. "Delicious venison, Julia," says Thomas Barnett, the owner of The Tuscaloosa Cotton Company. He dabs his mouth with a lace napkin.

"I enjoyed your column about the afterlife," Mrs. Jameson says to Jackson Cliff, editor of the newspaper. "And I'm very sorry you lost your mother."

Clara jabs me in the ribs. "I know Jackson Cliff's mother! She said she'd soon be visiting him. He was her favorite child."

Even in the new life, Clara is still the most gregarious person I've ever known.

Mrs. Jameson whispers to Mr. Cliff, "You know, Mr. Cliff, the veil between life and death is assuredly thin. There are times I'm sure I've heard Isaac's voice." She

216

puts a finger to her eye to wipe a tear. "Oh, I miss him so."

Julia, Clara, and I, see Colonel Jameson lean forward to stroke his wife's face. Then, he turns to Julia. "Your husband is such a treasure, my dear. Promise me that you'll cherish him for the rest of his days, for he needs you terribly in order to be as he once was."

Julia has heard what she needed to hear. "I will cherish him, Colonel." She gazes at Joseph, recalling the tender slide of his fingers on her skin, and the soothing sound of his voice when he first admitted his love for her. Oh, how she cherished him then—before he became so brooding—when he was *as he used to be*, fresh and new and innocent.

But—and Clara and I know this—Julia's impression of him, then, was obscured, made during a time when Joseph tried hard to stamp back the fire of his torment. Would she have fallen in love with him if he hadn't done so?

Mrs. Jameson is taking a handkerchief from her bosom. Mr. Cliff lays a sympathetic hand on her arm and whispers. "There, there, Mrs. Jameson. Our loved ones never really leave us, do they?"

Hattie crosses the room to her mother's chair, but Julia is unaware. "Why can't Mama see me?" Hattie asks Clara.

Clara touches Hattie's hair. "She doesn't need to see you. Your mother is going to be fine now. It's your father you've been sent to see. To be seen by. Are you ready to give him the gift?"

"Yes," Hattie says proudly.

"You've taught her well," I say to Clara, and she smiles.

"Then go give it to him, darling," Clara tells Hattie. "You see how distraught he is."

So Hattie calls out to Joseph, "Find your buried treasure, Daddy. Find me!" Then she runs into the hall.

At once, Joseph drops a crystal goblet of wine. It tumbles from the table to the oak-board floor of the dining room and bursts into pieces. At first, he doesn't move, staring at the tiny, red-tinged fractures of glass, and seeing in every piece, the face of his daughter. Then his eyes turn to Julia.

She takes charge and rings the little bell next to her plate for Noah. He comes quickly to sweep up the glass. "I got it, Miss Julia. Ya'll just go on with the dinner. It'll be cleaned up in no time."

"Oh, my," Clara says unhappily. "I hope it isn't beyond repair." She's still a little covetous of her crystal.

From the hall, Hattie calls again, "Daddy, come find me!"

Joseph rises, jolting the table. The guests stop talking and turn their attention to him, and he is frightened by their questioning eyes. These people do not know that he was once quite mad. If the terrors come upon him, he will cause Julia irreversible embarrassment. Yet he must follow Hattie. "Excuse me, I'll be only a moment," he says, glancing at Julia.

"What is it, darling?" she asks. He can tell from her contented expression that she's not heard Hattie's voice.

218

"Nothing really. It's just—. There's something I have to retrieve." He turns to address the inquiring eyes encircling the table. "A treasure for my wife. I must get it now. Please continue."

"How lovely. A gift for Julia, our beautiful hostess," Thomas Barnett says, his tone wooden, as though he knows he cannot divert everyone's attention. The chatter of voices and the clinking of silver against porcelain recommence.

Clara and I follow Joseph into the hall. His face is damp with perspiration, his voice, timorous. "Hattie?" He leans against the large, four-door, mahogany armoire that holds the coats of his guests, and repeats her name —no longer as a call, but as a cry for forgiveness. And then, a door of the armoire opens. Nestled between the wool, velvet, and herringbone coats that keep his guests safe from the outside cold—is his child. Joseph's vigor fails him. He sinks to his knees, like an old and hungry beggar, in front of her. He wants to push back the overcoats, to reach out and touch her, except he doesn't have the strength. And more, he fears her reaction. His touch, his fingers closing around her neck—is that the last earthly thing she remembers.? Or is she only a mirage, just the start of another terror in his mind? *Please Hattie, forgive me!*

So, the child reaches out *for him*, her slender fingers touch his hands like salve on an open wound.

"I *have* forgiven you, Daddy." She settles herself within his arms, against his chest, beneath his chin, contented. And looks up at him. "Don't you know I still love you?"

Joseph embraces her, as he used to. She is warm on his chest, flesh and blood in his arms. He can almost feel her heart beating. If only it *could* be as it once was, he is thinking, when he enjoyed the pleasure of Julia, of his children.

Clara is watching the two of them cling to each other, her head to one side, her lips pressed tightly together, trying not to cry--it's what she does when she's deeply moved. I give her arm a squeeze.

"You've done a fine job with your reparations, sweetheart," I say to my wife.

"But I've not finished, Francis." She motions for Hattie, her voice rising to a lilt. "Shall we complete our task, little one?"

Hattie moves from her father's embrace and steps into a shadowed corner of the hall. She returns holding the hand of a man with shoulders so stooped, he appears stricken and old, yet his face is no older than Joseph's. He wears the uniform of a Union soldier.

Joseph narrows his gaze, first on the uniform, then on the man, a man with creased lines across his forehead as if every troublesome moment of his life lay in stripes for all to see. His eyes, tired and murky as old water in Esther's wash bucket, are set on Joseph. *But this is a trick. The man wears a mask.* Behind the rippled forehead, behind the feeble eyes, is the despicable sergeant who nearly killed him in the prison camp. Joseph's own forehead tightens into lines, his own eyes become like sludge. Why is the man here with Hattie? And how can she be here at all, when she is dead? Dead and buried. Has she . . . she has . . . crossed the rings of time. Has she brought back the devil to punish him for what he did to her?

She's looking at him, now, with anticipation. She is standing beside the soldier, and waiting—for what? Moments ago, she said she forgives him, but now, his mind is filled with doubt—how could she? He must confront the evil that stands before him, and takes a step forward, but he draws back, wincing as if from another blow to his head. The soldier beside Hattie repulses him now as much as in the prison camp. The sergeant had nearly killed him. Joseph's head is pounding. The terrors are coming. He clinches his fists, and feels the burn of sin within his own hands, remembering Hattie's cries, her face turning blue, her body going limp in his arms, and, at last, his own howl of horror when he realized what he'd done.

The soldier smiles—is it a cynical smile? How dare he scoff at him! No, surprisingly, the man's smile is, not contemptuous, but rather beseeching, nearly humble. And now the devil speaks of forgiveness. "I know a little mercy is a lot to expect of you," the soldier says, looking down at the pine plank floor.

Joseph's entire countenance twists in loathing. "Mercy? I received no mercy. You beat me, starved me, and tortured me into a madness that caused me to do evil to my own daughter!" His thoughts return to his hand closing around the neck of his child. He knows Hattie is remembering, too; her look of love has shifted to one of disparagement. *Please Hattie, forgive me.*

Clara tenses beside me, is clasping and unclasping her hands—what she does that when she's worried. Her plan doesn't seem to be working. "Francis, what can I do?"

I put an arm around her shoulder, crushing her puff sleeve. She sloughs off my arm and rearranges the silk folds. "Can't you think of something? You're good at pushing things along. "

"You can't push someone to forgive."

"Then Hattie's death will plague Joseph forever. His hallucinations will not go away, and that is dangerous for Julia, and for him. Oh Francis, she wants things *as they used to be.*"

Being careful of her silk sleeves, I tug her closer. "Clara, my darling, you know Julia; what she wants is not realistic."

Clara lifts her chin. "Francis, *do not* underestimate Julia." And her worried gaze closes in on Joseph, the soldier, and Hattie, standing sullen and silent in the hall.

"Alright, for now, let's think of the three of them as our hypothetical triangle, almost perfect, except the sides are not quite closed."

"Francis, that is entirely too technical; too, too much like . . . a man. Think of something else."

"But our triangle needs only a single stroke to—"

"Sh-sh-sh!"

The only sound now, is the ticking of the clock. A Grandfather clock with its scrolled pediment, and the perfectly circular picture of a contented child on the top of the dial.

At that precise moment, Julia's unexpected laugh comes from the dining room, a resounding laugh, the same laugh that tumbled from her as a child after she'd re-sewn the ripped arm of a beloved rag doll, restoring it with Clara's needles, and her grandmother's step-by-step directives.

•

A smile from Hattie, and exhilaration. "Oh, Mama is just as I remember her now," Hattie says. "Did you hear her laugh, Daddy? It's just as it used to be."

He'd heard the laugh. It had stunned him, struck him in the very center of his chest, and then like a magnet, yanked him toward her, even more than when he saw her, tonight, coming down the stairs, looking as she used to. He wants to go back to her. He wants to be with Julia. But without being truthful, for like him, she no longer has the merciful heart of a child. He'll blanket his sin as he's used to, and continue to put up with the terrors, until he can bear them no more.

His eyes move to the Grandfather clock, to the perfect, circular picture of the child on its face, and then to the face of his own child, Hattie. He sees her innocence, her goodness, her smile of forgiveness. But she does not move toward him, or linger in his studied gaze. She takes her place, again, beside the stooped, repentant man who asked for his mercy, and received none. She is holding his rejected hand when they fade into the shadows of the hall.

Clara takes a deep-drawn breath. "I have failed, Francis. I didn't tidy things up as I meant to."

I kiss her forehead. "Let's not worry over it, my love. Let's leave that to Julia. Remember, we shouldn't underestimate our granddaughter."

Clara gives me another poke in the ribs and a kiss on my neck, then we notice Colonel Jameson entering the hall. "Oh there you are, Colonel,' Clara says.

The Colonel puts a hand on Joseph's shoulder, as if he will hear him. "Exquisite dinner party, Joseph. But time has lengthened to the ghostly hour of my departure. Once again, I thank you for my life those years ago, and say farewell, my good friend."

We move down the shadowed hall, where pictures of the dead hang from brass hooks on rosewood walls. From the dining room, we hear Julia cheerfully call out to Joseph, "What is keeping you, darling? Mr. Jameson has already left, and the rest of our company is waiting for you to bring my little treasure, whatever it might be."

Thomas Barnett's lighthearted voice follows. "Yes, you've been long enough, my good man. Retrieve your treasure and bring it. By now, it had better be something out of this world. Something truly extraordinary for our Julia!"

The End

43425482R00133

Made in the USA
Lexington, KY
29 July 2015